A HIGHLAN

BY

RICHARD F JONES

Also by Richard F Jones
A Flight Home
Dancing with the Devil
Time On Their Hands
Mountain Intrigue
War to the Death
Ben's Beach
Gabriella
A Highland Life
To the Top and Back Again
Doing It My Way
The Road to Freedom
Escape to Scotland
Explosive Voyage

To my wife Meg whose tireless efforts made the publication of this book possible.

©2024 Second Edition Richard F Jones. All rights reserved. Without limiting the rights under copyright reserved above, no part of this book maybe reproduced, stored in or introduced into a retrieval system, or transmitted, in any form, or by any means (electrical, mechanical, photocopying, recording, or otherwise) without the written permission of both the copyright owner and the above publisher of this book.

This is a work of fiction. Names, characters, places, brands, companies, media and incidents are either the product of the author's imagination or are used fictitiously. The author acknowledges the trademarked status and trademark owners of various products referenced in this work of fiction, which have been used without permission. The publication/use of these trademarks is not authorised, associated with, or sponsored by the trademark owners.

PROLOGUE

My dear, darling Anne I've been thinking about you a great deal recently, but now you're dead and gone I know I have to move on. The Ardnamurchan peninsular in the Western Highlands of Scotland which we used to visit is calling me back. The wildness, the silent mountains and lochs are echoing to my every fervent cry. Recently I've managed to lose the friends I needed losing and found others along the way. I've kissed the ladies and shaken hands to say my goodbyes, but I know I am going somewhere where my mind will be free to wander in the wind. But please don't ever become a stranger to me for that would make me very sad.

Sitting here in my empty room my path is clear to leave, but regrettably I know it will be without you. Hopefully the Ardnamurchan peninsula will provide me with the only alternative I'll ever want.

CHAPTER ONE

One day I was awoken in the middle of the night by hammering on my front door and ringing of the front doorbell. Looking at my bedside clock it told me it was somewhere about half past one. 'What the heck is all that about,' I thought. I went to the bedroom window and was amazed by what I saw outside. On the road and in my driveway I saw a host of police cars all with their blue lights flashing. I put on my dressing gown and went downstairs. On my way through the hallway I spotted more police officers outside my back door. 'For Christ's sake what's happening,' I said to myself as I walked to open the front door.

When I opened it four policemen barged in. Two of them grabbed hold of me and the other two carried on past me inside my house.

'What's all this about?' I said to the two who held onto me.

'We are taking you in for questioning,' one of them said. 'You've been accused of molesting a woman.'

'What!' I cried out. 'Utter nonsense.'

However, they made me get dressed, then I was handcuffed and bundled into the back of one of the police cars before driving off to the police station, leaving the other police officers to carry on with what looked like a ransacking of my house.

CHAPTER TWO

I am lying in bed when four young women dressed in what I would have called Victorian nightdresses appeared at my bedside. They all wore pretty pink nightcaps dating from the same era. Two of them were attractive, two of them were not. From different sides of the bed they all tried to get under the sheets with me, but somehow I managed to shove them all off. Then I must have fallen back into another deep sleep. Later on I could hear another rustling sound alongside my bedside. When I looked, a tall demure brunette wearing what looked like a pale blue riding coat was standing over me, waiting to get onto my bed. Reaching out to pull her towards me resulted in falling out of the bed and hurting my shoulder badly when I landed awkwardly on the floor.

The pain, on impact, woke me. It had all been a dream, or a nightmare and that's how it had been each night for many weeks. My nights sleep always ending in a similar manner, with similar crazy dreams, although fortunately I didn't always end up on my bedroom floor.

Anne and I had been in school together and after much and constant asking on my part, over a few school terms, I did manage to persuade her to become my girlfriend. At first it didn't go well as she rightly soon realised that I was a bit of a twit. However in time I did calm down and she began to put up with me. In fact during that time we ended our virginity together, although our early attempts produced more hilarity than passion. Our break-up occurred when she went off to Manchester University. My A-level results were not good enough for university purposes, whereas she obtained distinctions in every subject. Then the thought of her cavorting around in Manchester with scores of sex mad young men in term time was more than I could cope with. It was my decision to call off our relationship which didn't please her so we never spoke or communicated again during her time there.

When I left school I got a job as a junior reporter, and, after University, I found out that she went off to London to earn a fortune working for a city bank. Our paths then never crossed for nearly another ten years.

Then one day I was walking down Queen Street, the main shopping street in the centre of Cardiff, when I spotted this most gorgeous looking woman walking towards me. My eyes immediately stood out on stalks. By then I was working as a senior reporter for the Western Mail and had acquired the reputation of being a bit of a ladies man. I certainly enjoyed romping in bed with many of them. As I grew closer I realised it was Anne. She had certainly grown in the glamorous stakes though. Her black, shiny hair was down to shoulder length, her face obviously contained make-up and eye liner and heavy lipstick. She was wearing an expensive sheepskin coat, black tights and a short dark skirt. She had changed from a school girl into a fabulous looking mature woman and I instantly fancied her like mad.

'Anne,' I said when she was virtually in front of me. For a moment she stared blankly at me, for I suppose in outward appearance I had also changed radically. Gone were the scruffy clothes and jeans I used to wear when I was her boyfriend. So was the spotty face and unkempt hair I was blessed with. In their place was a white shirt and tie, smart dark suit and my hair was in a tidy modern lengthy style. It wasn't till I smiled that she recognised me.

'Gareth!' she responded eventually. 'I'm sorry I didn't recognise you.'

'Well you certainly look beautiful. How are you?'

'I'm fine,' she said.

'The last I heard you were working in London?' I continued.

'The bank I work for now has a large branch down here and I have moved back here to take charge of a section.'

'You mean here in Cardiff?' I asked.

'Yes,' she replied.

'That's great.'

We talked a bit more, briefly, about our respective families. 'Let me buy you a cup of coffee?' I asked, hoping to continue our conversation.

'I really should be getting back to work,' she said. 'This is my lunch hour.'

'Oh only for ten minutes. After all this time surely you can spare me that. Even if it's for old times sake.'

She hesitated. I was praying she would agree. 'Oh OK, but only for ten minutes,' she said. I pointed to the nearest coffee shop which was only twenty yards away.

When we sat down at a small round table I could see how truly beautiful she had become. When she took off the sheepskin coat I could take in the full majesty of her figure. She was stunning from head to toe. As fast as I could I asked her many questions about what she had been up to over the last ten years. Our two coffees went down fairly quickly. She then made motions that she was going to have to leave soon, 'Or I will be late back,' she said.

'I thought you were in charge?' I responded.

'You don't know what banking is like these days. Big Brother is always watching,' she said with a chuckle. When her face lit up like that it made her look even more beautiful, so I just couldn't let our meeting go that briefly. As I have mentioned, at that time, I was fairly confident with women.

'I'd like to ask you out for dinner one evening?' I said. 'There's so much more I'd like to know about what you've being doing. Please?' I added.

'Oh Gareth I don't know. What we had together was all a long time ago. I have a permanent boyfriend now.'

'My intentions would be purely platonic,' I responded. 'We did have some good times together and I'd like to reminisce on them and tell you about what I've been doing. I promise I shall keep my hands to myself.' That brought another smile from her.

After much coercion I managed to get her to agree to a time and date one evening to meet up. She agreed to that then ummed and ahhed about me collecting her from her house, but then she agreed to that after much persuasion by me. 'It will all be my treat,' I said trying to emphasise my commitment. So we made our farewells on the outside steps of the coffee bar and I walked away with a smug look on my face.

During the intervening days I arranged a dinner booking at one of my favourite expensive Italian restaurants. I usually only ate there when it was on the newspaper's expense account. I also arranged for my best suit and shirt to be laundered and bought a new pair of shoes, which for once matched my suit trousers. I also purchased a new bottle of Armani splash on, which I intended to liberally apply to my face and body.

I felt pleased with myself that I had discovered her home address. It was an upmarket nineteenth century, three storey terraced house, in a fashionable area near to the city centre. I speculated that it had cost substantially more than my three bed roomed semi in the suburbs of the city.

After I rang on her doorbell I was almost knocked out with what I was confronted with when she opened her front door to greet me. A short sheepskin jacket struggled to conceal a skimpy black dress that exemplified all the contours of her body. Having escorted her around my car to the passenger door I was privileged to a have a view of her nubile legs, right up to her thighs, as they twisted into the passenger seat.

On entering the restaurant the male waiters nearly fell over each other in a race to reach her and help her off with her jacket, then assist her onto the dining chair to reveal acres of nubile flesh under the skimpy black dress. If nothing else she was dressed to kill.

I could see her eyes light up when they settled on the expensive varied a la carte menu. 'This looks very good Gareth,' she said.

'Only the best for you,' I replied.

I ordered the chicken escalope and she chose the Dover sole. When the waiters finally left us alone, after making a big fuss of her, we were both able to sip on a glass of Chablis. 'Well it's great to see you again after all this time,' I toasted and we clinked our glasses together.

Whilst we devoured the whitebait we had ordered for our starters I began my interrogation into her recent history. In between the lines of what she said I gathered that she had enjoyed a whale of a time in Manchester and London as a single woman. She even admitted that she decided that she had to 'to calm down a bit,' since she had returned to Cardiff, as she didn't want to upset her parents who lived close by and were getting older. She was also becoming worried about their deteriorating health. The first bottle of Chablis was consumed before our main course arrived. I was glad I had brought plenty of cash with me as these were the days before credit cards. Having loosened her tongue I was able to discover that her current boyfriend was a bit of a boffin in finance, and they had met at a seminar on the subject. It transpired that they both stayed in their own houses as he needed time in peace and quiet to undertake his research. She told me that they usually co-habited at weekends and occasionally embarked on a continental week abroad. To me it didn't sound as though it was a passionate relationship.

Our time together over that meal positively raced by. The more we talked the more animated her exposed bodily movements became, the more I began to fall in love with her again. In fact by the end of the meal I realised that I had never really stopped loving her since we had parted all those years ago. There had been various other short term relationships, sometimes for a month or two, which with the benefit of hindsight I would describe as no more than amorous affairs. Indeed some of them were with married women, which I am not particularly proud of. It seemed our meal was over in a flash and I was receiving the bill from the over attentive waiters long before I had a chance to tell her much about what I had being doing. Driving back to her home we were able to continue with our dialogue right to her front door.

'I have enjoyed tonight Gareth,' she said when I stopped the car. 'Would you like to come in for a coffee?'

Wild horses wouldn't have kept me from accepting her invitation. The inside of her house looked most impressive, although my attention was more on her nubile body when she again removed her jacket, rather than the surrounding decor. I instantly realised that this was going to be my last opportunity to get into her psyche again. Next day I thought she could be back with her boyfriend and any chance I may have of rekindling our relationship would have gone, so I had to grasp the opportunity while it presented itself.

'Anne I am still desperately in love with you,' I said to her when we were standing looking straight at each other, a foot or two apart in the centre of her large lounge. 'You are still the most beautiful woman I've ever known,' I added. We moved into each others arms, our lips met for the first time in over ten years. Then our tongues intertwined. 'Anne I desperately want to make love to you,' I said with passion, when we came up for breath. I'm afraid we never got round to drinking the promised cup of coffee.

The hour we spent together in her bed was as passionate an entanglement as I had ever experienced. From the moans and groans she emitted from her mouth and the shudders that emanated from her body I could tell that I had satisfied her. We kissed our farewells in her downstairs hallway, with her attired only in her flimsy dressing gown while my hands took one last opportunity to explore the curvaceous contours of her body. 'I'll be in touch soon,' I said as I went out through the front door. She made no reply, but when I drove away in my car I shouted out 'Yes,' and pumped my fist in the air in celebration.

That night our encounter filled my dreams, but when I woke in the morning I knew if I wanted to get back in truck with her again I would have to follow it up quickly. I guessed she would expect me to phone, but I wasn't going to leave that to chance. If I did phone I expected her to say that she had to be a good girl and go back to her boyfriend. So I left it a day and then next evening I took a chance. Now knowing where she lived, at about half past seven I drove to her house and parked outside. There was a BMW two seater sports car parked outside which I guessed was hers. Quietly I walked up to the front door, peered in through the stained glass aperture, and spotted a light on inside, so I rang the doorbell. I knew I had the cheek of the devil, her boyfriend could be there inside with her. She opened the door and looked shocked when she saw me standing outside. She was wearing a white halter top which exemplified her breasts and tight blue denim jeans. That was all I needed as inspiration. 'Oh it's you,' she said. 'What do you want?'

'I thought we had such a wonderful time the other night that I'd like to make love to you again, please?'

For a moment she looked dumbfounded, but from the look on her face I could see I had stirred something in her memory. 'Well you're a nuisance I was watching something on the TV.'

'Well it's up to you,' I responded. She let me inside.

'Let me put it on record,' she said then went back into the lounge, where I could see the TV. I shut the front door then saw her fiddle about with her TV remote. Afterwards without saying another word she led me up the stairs to her bedroom, where she removed the halter top to reveal no bra, then the jeans and knickers and we continued where we had left off previously, only this time we kept at it for two hours. Again we parted inside her hallway with her only wearing the same flimsy dressing gown, while our lips and tongues intertwined. I repeated my parting shot of, 'I'll be in touch.' She again said nothing in reply, but it appeared that her arms held onto me for a shade longer.

After that encounter I really considered I was getting somewhere with her. In our prolonged sexual indulgence I got the feeling that for her, it was more than just the thrill of a one night stand. She used my name on several occasions in an endearing manner. Where did I go from there with her though was my next dilemma. I wanted her for more than just the sex.

As before I held my fire for a couple of days. I still didn't want to push my luck too far and frighten her off. I waited until the Saturday for the next visit to her house. Again I was taking a chance and pushing my luck. She had previously told me that she and her boyfriend used to shack up together for the weekend and I wondered if he might be there with her or she with him at his place. But again my luck was in. She opened the front door and on this occasion there was almost a welcoming look on her face when she invited me in. She was alone inside. It was half past one in the afternoon.

'I don't know that I am doing the right thing in all this,' she said as we stood facing each other in her lounge. This time I took in some of the décor. There was an expensive leather settee and two armchairs and a thickly piled carpet. 'I am supposed to be seeing Brian for dinner tonight and then go back to his place.'

'Well, I would never want to force you into anything,' I replied. 'I care about you too much to do that. It's just that I'm afraid I have fallen in love with you all over again. I can't help how I feel. If you tell me to go I will go without making a fuss or a scene.'

'Oh I see,' she said. 'It will be my turn to do that this time will it.'

'I never meant it like it seemed,' I replied. 'I was just jealous. I couldn't bear the thought of you being with all those other young men students in Manchester. I couldn't have coped with just seeing you at the end of term time.'

'I see,' she said.

I moved towards her and pulled her into my arms. She didn't object. We again kissed passionately. 'Please can I make love to you,' I said.

She took me by the hand and again led me up to her bedroom.

This time though there were no holds barred between us. She was on top of me as much as I was on top of her.

'Christ, look at the time,' she hollered after we had both yet again reached another climax. The bedside clock showed six o'clock 'I'm supposed to be seeing Brian in just over an hour. I've got to shower and do my hair. You'll have to go, and quick,' she said then leapt out of the bed still naked and walked to the bedroom door for her dressing gown. The view I was treated to was worth being there on its own, let alone what had taken place between us before. She turned and faced me as she put on the dressing gown. For a few moments I had a full frontal as well, then she said. 'Gareth Rees you've always led me into trouble. You started me off on all this sex malarkey.' I was then summarily dismissed and told to make my own way out of the house. This time there was no goodbye kiss for me in her hallway. By the time I reached the front door I could already hear the shower running.

* * * * *

This time I didn't push my luck by contacting her next day. In fact it was Anne who telephoned me on the Sunday. She didn't sound in a good mood. 'Gareth I just don't know what to do about us,' she said before I had a chance to say anything.

'What do you mean?' I responded.

'I had a terrible time with Brian last night. I felt awful. I had to pretend I had a bad stomach. I hardly ate much of my meal and I drove home alone to my house after it. I just couldn't face going to bed with him after what I had done with you in the afternoon.'

'Well what do want to do about it?'

'At this moment I don't know. It's too early to decide. All this thing with you has happened so fast. I just wasn't prepared for it. You'll have to give me time to think.'

'Ok,' I said. 'I've already said that I care for you too much to push you into anything you don't want to do.'

'Gareth I would be grateful if you would leave me alone for a while to sort myself out. If you call at my house, I either won't answer the door if I know it's you, or I won't let you in if I open it by mistake. And if you phone me I'll put the phone down when I hear your voice. You'll have to wait for me to phone you. Will you agree to that?'

I hesitated for a few moments before replying. 'Ok,' I eventually responded. 'But when you do decide, will you please let me know what your decision is. I just couldn't bear not knowing without hearing it directly from you. Whatever, I want you to know that I will always love you and I guess I always have.'

'Thank you,' she said. 'I promise I will let you know one way or another.'

'Thank you,' I said and we ended our call. For some time afterwards I sat staring out of the window of my lounge, doing nothing in particular but thinking about all the times we had spent together.

But that's how I left it. A part of me still wondered if I would ever hear from her again. At the very most I thought I might receive a 'Dear John' letter. I mean what did she want to bother long term with me for. This guy Brian was obviously a far cleverer bloke than me, another university graduate I was told and from what she mentioned he was also far wealthier than me. He owned a house in Llandaff, very similar to hers, but situated in a far more affluent and upmarket area. It was where all the 'nobs' lived.

So I was more than surprised when on the following Thursday I received a telephone call from her. 'Gareth,' she began, 'I still haven't definitely made up my mind about us, but I do need to see you to talk about it.'

'Good,' I responded, almost before she had finished the sentence.

'I'm not going to see you at my house or yours. I will meet you for a coffee and a sandwich in town, one lunch time. But only for an hour as I'll have to get back to work.'

'Excellent,' I responded. We agreed on a venue for one o'clock the next day.

'This time the lunch is on me,' she added.

'Even better,' I replied.

Again on the day I made sure I put on a fresh clean shirt and respectable suit. We met outside at our agreed rendezvous. She again wore the sheepskin coat and another short, this time, blue skirt. We greeted each other affectionately, but there was no passionate kiss or embrace. She did however present her cheek to me and I was allowed to kiss that. We went inside and ordered coffee and sandwiches for two.

'Thank you for seeing me,' I said as an opening gambit. Underneath the sheepskin coat she was wearing a white blouse open at the neck and a blue cardigan which matched the skirt.

'Did you think I wouldn't?' she responded.

'Well knowing my experiences with other women I did wonder.'

'But surely you must know I am not one of your other women, however many there may have been.' I caught her looking at me with that knowing look which was part of her response when she was dealing with me, which I had come to know so well from our time together before.

'Quite right,' I said. We both picked up one of the sandwiches and bit into them, then I let her do the talking.

'As I said on the phone I'm still not exactly sure what to do about all this. I repeat it's all come upon me so quickly and I wasn't prepared for it, so it's going to take me time to come to terms with it,' she said. 'Before I do anything more with you I have to square it with Brian. He's done me no harm and I have to treat him tactfully. Perhaps I realise that what I had with him wasn't enough or I wouldn't have got involved with you as I have done.' I nodded my head in understanding as I continued to chew on my sandwich. 'Heaven knows,' she continued. 'I've had enough sex in my life to know that it wasn't just that that appealed to me about you.' I again nodded my head. No way was I going to interrupt her.

'Can I ask you a few pertinent questions?' she asked next.

'Fire away,' I replied. 'Ask me what you want.'

'If we make a go of our relationship, would you want to marry me?'

'I'd marry you today,' I responded. She laughed which made her look gorgeous.

'If we married would you want children?'

'If they all looked like you, without doubt.' Again she sniggered.

'Ok,' she said and supped on her coffee. 'You see that is the thing about Brian. He's so wrapped up in his work that he doesn't want to get married. He's happy with our relationship as it is, because it fits in with his work. And he has already told me that there is no way he would want to have children around him interfering with all of that.'

'Seems to me like I'm your man then.' I said. 'Maybe the last resort, but perhaps it better than nothing.'

She stuck her tongue out at me. That was something else I hadn't witnessed for a long time, but it made her look rude and gorgeous.

After a short while she brought our luncheon meeting to a conclusion, stating that the hour was nearly up and she had to get back to work. Prior to paying the bill she said, 'Thank you Gareth. I still don't know what to do for the best, but I promise you I will give you my decision as soon as I can. I can't say any more.'

We parted with me giving her a kiss on the other cheek, but I walked back to work still not really knowing where I stood with her.

* * * * *

Another week or more passed and I had nothing more to do than to brood on the state of helplessness she had left me in. I knew I couldn't push it, so a lot of the time I just wallowed in my despair. There were many occasions when I wondered if it was worth putting myself through all this hell, then I thought about the way she looked, the way her face crinkled when she laughed and smiled and her normal good hearted cheer when we were having fun together.

Then on a weekday, I couldn't remember which day it was, she phoned me at work.

'Are you all right?' she asked.

'Fine, except for missing you,' I replied.

'Good,' she responded.

'Well if you still want to I'm am happy for you to ask me out on a date if that's what you'd like.'

For a moment I was gobsmacked and I couldn't think of a suitable response. She interrupted by saying, 'You don't have to if you don't want to.'

'No, no, no,' I responded instantly. 'Yes please,' I added. My mind was still in a turmoil so I asked what everybody else did in those days on their first date and suggested we go to the cinema. She agreed and we arranged a time and date. She said she would make her own way there and would drive herself home. She added that if I was going to make a fuss about that she wouldn't meet up with me at all. To this day I haven't a clue what film it was and what it was about, but just to sit there alongside her in a normal situation was all I could possibly want. During the interval I bought choc ices for us and afterwards we went for a coffee in a nearby café, then, as couples did in those days we drove home separately.

Our courtship, along those lines continued for a few weeks. I was re-introduced to her parents. Her mother treated it like the return of the prodigal son. She had given birth to two daughters. Whenever I went there I was served my food on the best china. One time when attending for a meal with them, her father was forced to say, 'Look I pay all the bills here. Why is it that whenever he comes he's given the largest portion.' Her mother was forced to cover herself with embarrassment. Anne later revealed to me that one day she went home for tea when I wasn't with her, but her mother still laid out the best tea service. Her father remarked that he hadn't been told that, 'Gareth was coming to tea today,' which of course I wasn't.

After a few weeks Anne and I had settled on getting married sometime in the following year. Anne then suggested that we should stay celibate until we were married. 'It will give us something to look forward to,' she said. Unfortunately, by then my frustration of seeing her regularly, looking so sexy and attractive was causing me to burst at the seams with frustration. I'm afraid to say to say that her pronouncement lasted about three days before we passionately succumbed to our joint sexual desires. Thereafter, we indulged in a similar relationship as she had with Brian, wherein we lived together at the weekend, usually at her place, as it was more salubrious and comfortable than my bachelor pad.

Then tragedy struck. In the middle of the night when I wasn't there she was in writhing pain and had to call out the ambulance to take her to hospital. It transpired that she had a twisted bowel which required immediate surgery. However there were unexpected complications and she died in the hospital three days later. During that time I only managed to see her once and even then she was in a coma.

CHAPTER THREE

To escape all the hell that followed her death that led to the early morning call of the police, which I'll describe in detail later on, I packed up my job as newspaper reporter in Cardiff, sold my home there and moved lock, stock and barrel, for peace of mind and tranquillity, to the Western Highlands of Scotland.

One day in my newly acquired Highland bungalow I was struggling to reach the ceiling, attempting to apply white emulsion paint onto its scratchy surface. Only possessing one small pair of steps the continual stretching upwards caused my arms to ache. The shoulder I had fallen on when falling out of bed the previous night during my dream of all the girls in their night dresses, hurt badly. A more elaborate pole length brush was required, but that would entail a trip to Fort William some forty miles away.

I had moved into that small bungalow about a month before on a long term let and had been able to negotiate a reduced rent on the condition that I redecorated the interior, which was badly needed in every room. Apart from that and the age and uncomfortable nature of the old fashioned furniture it provided an ideal bolt hole for me in the frame of mind I was in at that time. My nearest neighbour was about four hundred yards away and on the land in between us roamed a flock of sheep and four West Highland cattle. From my front window, when the clouds weren't hovering low, I could see the mountain range of Sgurr Dhòmhnaill and out of the side windows there was a view of the loch across which we all had to cross to get to Fort William.

It was then six months since Anne had died and I realised that the attractive black haired girl who was in my dreams the previous night was her. After her death I had a bit of a breakdown which resulted in me losing my job as a newspaper reporter. But more of that later. At that moment I had enough problems applying sufficient paint to the ceiling with my painful left arm.

Later on I had to race down the steps to switch off the radio. I needed to slam my index finger down on the off button to obliterate the music. They were playing one of Anne's favourite songs. Hearing the melody blaring from the radio was too much for me to bear. Listening to something that was so familiar to both of us immediately instigated a bout of morbid depression. Instantly I could visualise her hair, her body and her long sexy legs. I had partly escaped to the highlands, as I hoped there would be nothing familiar there to remind me of her. It was then that I realised that the other girls in the previous nights dream were a mixture of other girlfriends I had rejected years before. When I eventually finished painting that particular ceiling I downed tools and decided I needed fresh air.

Fortunately in the highlands that is a commodity that is in constant abundance. Summer or winter, rain or shine, there are usually strong gusts coming in off the Atlantic. Long walks over the mountains and forests had become my attempted therapy, so I donned my windcheater, boots and whistled up my dog Bella who was nestled in her bed in the kitchen. I had acquired her from a nearby crofter who I had befriended since my arrival there. At his advanced age Bob had been unable to cope with the five dogs he already had. Bella was the youngest and therefore the most lively. By the time she joined me she was house trained and obedient off the lead. She had already begun her training of rounding up sheep, so when we were on our walks she would often round up anything that moved including falling leaves and sometimes to my embarrassment fellow walkers and hikers.

That day, for once, there was no rain about although in that area the distant clouds indicated that it was never very far away. We were taking a forestry track that led to the foothills of one of the bigger mountains. I was not planning to climb to the summit that day as it was at least a five mile hike and I still had to get back to my painting task. There was a breeze up and Bella was in and out of the verdant undergrowth and babbling streams adjacent to the path as we walked.

We had gone about a mile I guess, when suddenly something moving in the forest up ahead caught my attention. Often there were deer in that woodland. Initially I thought it was one of them. I stopped walking as I didn't want to frighten it. At that moment Bella was some way behind me. However the figure in the wood didn't move either, it just stood still behind a tree trying to keep out of sight. Then I realised it was a human, a small, very slight human being.

I moved slowly and called out 'hello'. The figure moved out from behind the tree, then stopped and stared at me. Tentatively I moved closer. Then I could see it was a girl or even perhaps a young man, I just couldn't distinguish which. It was the strangest human sight I had ever seen. The clothes worn were part cloths and part animal skins. On the head was something that was a cross between a beret and a bobble hat, yet it had spikes like knitting needles sticking out of its top. On the forehead there was the most amazing bright star like motif, either painted or tattooed on. Whatever, it was a very mind blowing creature.

I repeated my 'hello', which again produced no response. Unfortunately my calling out had alerted Bella who came racing to catch me up. When she was alongside she could sense the presence of someone near and began to bark. To stop her chasing off in that direction I grabbed hold of the dog's collar and made her sit beside me. To do that I had to look down at the dog. When I looked up again the being in the wood had disappeared. Bella and I continued on our walk and although I didn't see the person again that day it played on my mind.

* * * * *

The following evening Bella and I were returning from our late afternoon walk. On the track we had to pass the farmhouse cottage that belonged to Bella's former owners, Bob and Jessie. When I was near I liked to call in to see them as they were interested in my progress with Bella and also I tried to keep a check on them to see if they were well, or needed anything heavy lifted. I could hear Jessie in the outside shed where she used to keep their hens. She was in the process of feeding and locking them up for the night. She'd told me previously that the fox had taken a couple of them recently. Before I entered the shed I spotted inside a diminutive figure suddenly race out of the back door. Although it was dusk I was sure it was the being I had seen in the wood the previous day.

'There you are, strangers,' Jessie called out when she saw us. Bella ran to greet her and they made a fuss of each other. Jessie was a tiny wee woman in her seventies. She usually wore a housecoat overall and her grey hair was normally tied in a bun.

I explained that I had been busy with my redecoration and hence my recent absence from their company. 'Have you just had a visitor?' I asked when I'd completed my explanation.

'Oh yes that's Mhairi,' Jessie responded. 'She comes and goes like the wind. In fact she is as wild as the wind.'

'I thought I saw her in the wood the other day. She's a girl then is she?'

'Or a woman,' Jessie. 'Nobody knows just how old she is, nor does she, in fact. She's lived up in the mountains for as long as anybody here can remember, winter and summer. How she survives we don't know. We are one of the few people she will talk to, probably because of our animals. The dogs make an enormous fuss of her and even the sheep like her, but her English is limited which makes it difficult to converse and even then we don't understand half of what she says. We offer her food but she won't take it, except eggs.'

'Has she got a hut up there?' I asked.

'No. Bob knows every inch of that ground. In the summer he takes the sheep up there to graze but there is no hut or dwelling of any type anywhere. He thinks she lives in one of the caves, but where or which one, nobody knows.'

'Is Mhairi her full name?' I asked.

'We don't know what her real name is but that's what we call her and she responds to it. It means rebellious and obstinate which is what she is.'

After some more conversation I left Jessie to her chores and returned to my bungalow to deal with Bella's tea and my evening meal.

CHAPTER FOUR

A few days later I received a letter from my solicitors who were based in Cardiff, my home town in South Wales. One of the problems I had been involved with down there before I left for the Highlands was an alleged case of attempted rape by me, involving one of my female work colleagues at the newspaper offices where we had both been employed. As far as I was concerned the accusations were complete nonsense and a figment of the woman's imagination. The case against me had in fact already been dismissed due to lack of sufficient evidence to back up my accuser, Janet Lawrence's, story. Now, however, my solicitors said in their missive that there was new evidence that Janet had unearthed which the Crown prosecutor needed to investigate. I had worked with Janet Lawrence for about three years. She was a very attractive young woman in her early thirties with jet black, short wavy hair, a good figure and long legs and portrayed a somewhat sexy image in her attire. I suppose it would be fair to say that we were attracted to each other in a vibrant office type of way. At the time though I was very much involved with Anne and Janet had a boyfriend who she lived with. Occasionally though we would flirt with each other around the office desk and I guess sometimes I did put my arm around her waist, although it was completely in a platonic manner and she never objected, and that was as far as it went, as far as I was concerned. In our working environment there were many other similar dalliances but nobody took them particularly seriously. If anything it was more about relieving the tedium of the working day.

The problems with Janet started after Anne died. I think she could see how distraught I was so on a couple of occasions she took me out after work for a drink at a nearby pub. I agreed as I thought it was her intention to try and cheer me up.

Soon though it became obvious that her motives were more sexually orientated than that. She began to tell me how much she fancied me and wanted me to make love to her. I pointed out that she already had a boyfriend who she lived with.

'Oh that doesn't matter,' she responded curtly, 'we are only good friends really. I fancy you much more.'

I protested that it was too early for me to become involved with anybody else after Anne's recent death, but Janet paid no heed to my words. She continued to proposition me so I stopped going out for a drink with her. However she continued to harass me on the matter during the day, around the office. It came to point where I had to tell her to get lost. Then one day I received a call from my bosses, on the top floor, to go and see them about a 'serious personal matter.'

I was therefore both surprised and astonished when the editor, Clifford Johns and the assistant editor, Ben Howe, confronted me with Janet's complaint of sexual harassment against me.

'That's complete nonsense,' I responded while standing in front of them. Initially I was too gob-smacked to make much more of a reply.

Clifford Johns then held up the sheet of paper which obviously contained Janet's written complaint. He was a stocky man in his forties and was wearing a blue short sleeve shirt and yellow tie. In passing it over he said, 'We have to take this seriously Gareth. Janet Lawrence is a mature woman who has been working here for five years and in that time we have never had any doubt to question her intelligence or integrity.'

Before making any reply I read the missive. In it Janet wrote, naming me, that I had repeatedly manhandled her including touching her breasts on numerous occasions. She went on to say that I had also tried to kiss her bare neck many times. She concluded by saying that she had many times told me to stop such behaviour or she would report me, but that I had ignored her warning.

'This is a pack of lies,' I said while slapping my hand on the offending piece of paper. 'Firstly I have never tried to kiss her neck or handle her breasts. Very occasionally I may have put my arm around her waist, but it has never gone higher or lower, and then it was only as a gesture of friendship. I then went on to tell them about our few after work drinks together and the chat up line she gave me about us getting together sexually. 'If anything she is the one who has been harassing me,' I said. 'As you know it has been a tough time for me since Anne died.' I handed back the piece of paper and they both mumbled something unintelligible in response.

'Well do you want to make a claim against her?' Clifford Johns said.

'No, that would be stupid,' I replied. 'At the moment I have enough problems on my mind without going through all that nonsense.'

Johns and Howe both looked at me emphatically. 'Well we can't ignore it Gareth. As she has put it in writing we have to do something about it,' Howe cut in. 'Are you sure you don't want to make a counter claim?'

'No, not in my current state of mind. I repeat I just couldn't stand all that nonsense. I know I haven't done anything wrong.'

'Well we'll have to interview her to get her side of the events,' Clifford Johns said. The ceiling lights reflected on his shiny, bald head. 'We'll let you know the outcome, but in the meantime don't do anything silly, like having an argument with her. It would be best if you tried to keep away from her.

'That's what I have been trying do for the last couple of weeks,' I responded.

On that note we parted and I went back to my desk. That night, at home, the blues really set in on me. As a result I had too much to drink and in my stupor even called out to Anne, 'Where are you when I need you!' Next day I had a hangover and felt worse.

Later on, in the afternoon, I was called up again to the editor's suite. Johns and Howe were both sitting behind Johns large oval, paper strewn desk. This time I was asked to sit in a chair opposite them.

'Well Gareth we have interviewed Janet Lawrence and she is adamant that what she has written in her letter is an accurate account of what has taken place,' Johns said to me after I had sat down.

'She's telling a pack of lies,' I responded. 'As you both know Anne's death has left me in a very bad state and the thought of entering into any sort of liaison with any other woman at the moment is a complete anathema to me. I just wouldn't have the mental or the physical strength to deal with it.'

'Ok,' Johns responded. 'We appreciate that but we have no alternative to take the matter further, she will sue the newspaper if we don't.'

'What have you got in mind then?'

'I think it might be best if we suspend you from work for the time being. You'll remain on full pay until the investigation is complete.'

Hell's bells, I thought to myself that's the last thing I want. At that moment work and the company of my male work companions was all that was keeping me from going mentally ill. Spending long periods of time moping around my house all day by myself was the last thing I needed. 'That's not going to do me much good in my present condition,' I said to the two of them.

'I'm afraid we haven't really got any other choice.' Howe responded. 'Until an investigation is complete we can't have you working together. If you had made a counter complaint then we would have had to suspend her as well,' he added. They then said they would put it all in writing to me in a letter, outlining my rights, and the wrongs I had purported to undertake.

I argued some more but got nowhere. A security guard then accompanied me to my desk, and when I had collected my things from it he escorted me to the front door of the building. For better or for worse most of my colleagues were out of the office at the time so there was no-one around to commiserate with or moan to.

That evening I succumbed to the supposed sanctity of alcohol which did me no good at all as I had horrendous nightmares throughout my sleeping hours. In the morning I felt like death warmed up and later on the letter from my employers arrived which only added to my despair. It spelt out most of what they had said to me on the previous day but added that my suspension would last a month to enable the matter to be cleared up completely. That added to my gloom. The only saving factor was that I would remain on full pay for that period of time.

Again that evening I indulged myself in the whisky bottle, only this time my nightmares turned into reality, with the police hammering on my front door at one-thirty in the morning.

CHAPTER FIVE

Following my meeting with Jessie in her wood shed in the Western Highlands and the further sighting of the strange girl or woman I decided that just walking and undertaking my decorating tasks was not a sufficient remedy for my continued state of depression. I needed proper work and more contact with other people to help rid myself of those blues. Since my arrival there I had noticed that twice a day, once up and once back, Forestry commission Land Rovers hurtled along the narrow road outside my front gate. I knew that three or four miles away there was a large forestry woodland which stretched out across the land underneath Sgurr Dhòmhnaill. Also on my shopping trips to the village I had noticed a collection of Forestry Commission huts and offices. I decided to call in and see if there was any employment available.

I spoke with a robust well built Scot, McIntosh, who informed me that as they were approaching the planting season there could be jobs available. 'It will be all physical work though, planting trees and digging ditches,' he said. 'Have you done anything like that before?' I said I hadn't but I stated I was in reasonable physical condition.

'Ach, you look fit enough to me,' he replied. 'Can you lift a sack of coal?'

I didn't know if I could but I said yes anyway.

'Leave it with me,' he said. 'I'll speak to the chief about it. Call in on Monday and I'll let you know.'

So that was it. Instantly that conversation perked up my spirits. Over the weekend I thought if I was going to be working in forests and mountains I'd better get my legs into some form of shape and so decided next day to take the track to the summit of Sgurr Dhòmhnaill to give them a proper work out.

Bella and I set out early. At the end of a three mile forest track there was a gate, then we had to ford a small river which she loved, and I nearly fell in, before embarking on the narrow path that led to the peak. It was a long, arduous two hour trek on a rough steeply rising path. As we neared the summit we were both puffing profusely. Fortunately the day was clear and I was looking forward to the panoramic views from the top. Below us I could see the extent of the woodland I would probably be working in if I got the job with the commission.

To get up onto the summit itself we had to climb over a rugged outcrop of rock. When we scrambled onto the narrow plateau of the peak I was astonished to see the small woman I had seen running from Jessie's shed the previous day, squatting there on her haunches. She appeared to be smoking something that looked like a weed. She looked as though she was just as astonished to see us.

She got up quickly, but couldn't go very far, as the plateau was narrow and the only way down was past Bella and me. There was a sheer drop all around the rest of it.

'Hello,' I said, Bella barked.

The girl/woman nodded her head. She was wearing the same combination of skins and cloths as I had seen her in before. They were multicoloured, but mostly greens and browns. The same headgear with spikes sticking out the top was on her head. She was short, hardly five foot in height and as thin as a stick, but her most striking feature was the star like motif on her forehead, which was coloured red and gold. It held my attention for many moments. She held out her hand towards Bella who moved forward and licked it affectionately.

'Hello,' I repeated, 'I'm Gareth.'

She mumbled something in reply which I took to mean the word Mhairi, which Jessie had mentioned was her name.

'You live here?' I asked. She nodded her head in affirmation and pointed down below. Whatever she was smoking was still in her hand. It certainly wasn't a cigarette of any type.

She started to move past us. Bella made another fuss of her. 'Hang on we'll come down with you,' I said. I had a quick look at the views from the plateau but the woman had already begun to climb down over the outcrop of rocks so I had to move speedily. Pity, because having made the effort to get up there I had wanted to take in the whole panorama below. However, Bella was already following her. They were both too quick and agile for me and I was soon struggling to catch up.

Having to hurry caused me to constantly stumble. My language became worse as I continued. This is stupid I eventually thought and shouted out, 'Wait for me,' which caused them both to turn around and look up in my direction. 'Bella come here,' I added which she obeyed. However my words didn't stop Mhairi's progress. She continued on down the mountain getting further and further away from us with every skipping stride.

When we got further down the mountain to where it widened out I spotted her figure out to my left some quarter of a mile away, moving away from the downward path. I stood and watched her for some time. Bella had also spotted her and was whining constantly alongside me. As my eyes followed the nymph's progress I could see in the distance the entrance to a cave in the side of the mountain. She was obviously heading that way. By that time I was too tired to follow her. My legs were aching and we still had to cross the river which wouldn't be easy. I did however make a mental picture of the cave and vowed to be back there soon.

That evening I was exhausted and crashed out asleep after eating a meal. This time the whisky bottle wasn't needed to assist my relaxation. The long walk and meeting the girl had provided the remedy. Bella was also flat out alongside my bed. Neither of us stirred until dawn.

On the Monday morning I spotted McIntosh's forestry Land Rover pull up outside my front gate. I watched him walk up my driveway and I was waiting at my front door to greet him and invite him in.

'H'm this place looks better than when I last saw it. You've been busy,' he began. We exchanged pleasantries about the redecoration process, then he said, 'I've spoken to the chief. He's happy for you to start work with us. If you could come down to the office this afternoon there are a couple of forms to complete and we can fit you out with some gear.'

He re-emphasised that the work would be totally physical and would require some climbing of mountains and hills. I would be involved in the planting of trees. That afternoon I made my way down to the office and completed the necessary job application form. I was then fitted out with a pair of heavy duty forestry boots, a waterproof lined jacket with hood and a pair of waterproof trousers. 'You'd better have some midge cream as well,' he added handing me a jar of the stuff. 'They can be evil sometimes in the forest,' he said. I had already tasted the wee beasties ire when I had been gardening at my cottage so I knew what to expect in that respect.

'If you're willing you can start tomorrow morning,' he said to which I agreed. 'Ok then, the Land Rover will pick you up at seven thirty outside your front gate.'

* * * * *

I quickly discovered what a complete change in working lifestyle and conditions forestry work was in comparison to my previous journalistic occupation. I guess nothing had really properly prepared me for it. The journey in a cramped steamy Land Rover with six other large bodies over a treacherous mountain road at seven thirty in the morning was a shock to the system before you began to work. My working colleagues consisted of a few old lags who had lived and worked on the peninsular all their lives. Some of them had never been further than Fort William. The others were mostly young drop outs like me who had moved there for the change in lifestyle. By the odour on their forestry jackets it seemed that nearly all of the young ones smoked some kind of pot. By the time we got to our working destination I was usually quite high myself by just breathing in the surrounding aroma.

After leaving the Rover we then had to walk a mile or two and sometimes often up a thousand feet or more to the area of land where we would be working on that day. Then a long, back breaking tedious slog of a days tree planting would begin. The trees, mainly larch and sidka spruce were saplings about seven or eight inches in height which we planted in furrows that had been previously raised by a tractor. It was a long eight hour day and we only had half an hour for a lunch break or 'piece' as it is known up there, which we ate while sitting on the ground. The journey home in the Land Rover back over the mountain road just about crippled the parts of my body that hadn't already been crippled by the days work.

At home, while I lay in the bath trying to soak out the aches, I promised myself that I would never again moan about the working conditions in a newspaper office. After taking Bella out and eating a meal I could do little else but crash out on my bed, to try and rest and prepare myself for the following days punishment. By the end of the first week I really didn't think I would be able to cope with it. But somehow, as you do, when you have to, I gradually got fitter and more attuned to the work. Thankfully I was able to have a bit of a laugh about it all with the younger lads, although the older local guys were not impressed and thought we were all a spoilt bunch of little brats compared to the hardships they had needed to face throughout their working and their home lives. The biggest plus for me was that I was at least earning a wage which enabled me to keep my head above water financially.

Throughout this period of time though I was also having to cope with the mental pressure of what my solicitor back home had written to me about. They'd stated that Janet Lawrence had brought new evidence against me in her claim of rape, which the public prosecutor was considering. My legal people stated that it was likely I would have to go back down there to confront those details. If the prosecutor then decided I had a case to answer to I would have to face a trial. That was a situation I didn't want, not only for the obvious reason, but also having just started work I was reluctant to take time off so soon, as well as the cost of the journey. It was a dilemma that played on my mind throughout my working day. Thankfully at night I was too shattered to do anything but just crash out on my bed asleep.

One evening, after work on my walk with Bella I was talking to Bob and Jessie in their shed, when, to my surprise, Mhairi walked in. This time she didn't run away or totally ignore me. Jessie said to her, 'Hello Mhairi, this is our friend Gareth.' Again the star on her forehead shone out like a beacon. Bella ran to her and jumped up at her licking her arms and legs. The girl responded to her with affection. This time though there was a cursory nod of acknowledgement in my direction. The clothes and crazy headgear she wore were the same as before, but I noticed her feet were bare and her slim brown legs mainly exposed. 'Gareth lives in a bungalow further down the road and works for the forestry commission,' Jessie continued trying to exemplify my permanence to the locality.

Mhairi ignored her attempts to bring me into the conversation and responded to Jessie in a dialogue I had never heard or encountered before.

'Duplieupsom scrimple in the macrehanitious,' she began. What that meant or inferred I hadn't a clue, but Jessie seemed to understand her and replied, 'Well as long as you are OK that's fine.' They continued to talk in this incoherent gibberish for some moments while Bob and I conversed about the inclement weather and my work for the forestry commission. Eventually I had to leave.

Bella was pining for her tea and so was I. Mhairi continued to ignore me and talk to Jessie when I left them.

By the end of my second week in work my body was becoming more used to the planting, the challenging terrain and the weather. Gradually I was also beginning to enjoy the camaraderie (the craic) with the other younger lads whilst working in the peace and surroundings of that beautiful mountain scenery. Many times though during the day a beazer, a rainstorm, would set in. Where we worked there was no shelter and on those occasions we all ended the day like drowned rats. If we worked for more than three hours in continuous rain we were allowed to go home early. All in all the experience was beginning to provide the therapy for my addled mind, although my solicitors letter still sitting permanently on my sideboard at home continued to rankle. Unfortunately I kept putting off replying to it. I did consider ignoring it completely, but I knew if I did that the law would only come looking for me.

* * * * *

At the weekend my muscles had sufficiently attuned for me to consider a longer walk. Bella was also becoming frustrated by her lack of exercise. With me gone all day she only got a short walk in the morning before the Land Rover picked me up and then only a truncated one in the evening before tea. After that I was too shattered to do much else but take her around the garden for her last visit at bedtime. So, to satisfy both our needs I decided to make for Sgurr Dhòmhnaill again on the Sunday morning. This time I wasn't planning to go for the summit. My aim was to try and get to the cave that I saw Mhairi heading towards a couple of weeks back.

With the recent heavy rains crossing the swollen river presented a bigger problem than before as there were many mini rapids. I had to attempt three or four different crossing points before I eventually got over. Bella of course swam over and was waiting impatiently for me on the other side. It was then another hour before the track to the summit diverted off to the spot where I had seen Mhairi disappearing in the distance. That route was not really a track. The ground was rough shale and hardly worn away. How she managed it in her bare feet I couldn't understand. I was struggling in my forestry boots.

Gradually the cave came into view. As I got closer I could see smoke coming out through the entrance. I hoped that meant she was in there. I guessed if she was and sitting looking out she could easily see Bella and me approaching. The climb up to the entrance was very slippery. Loose rocks and shale caused me to regularly stumble and curse. No wonder nobody had found this place before, I thought. There was one last scramble, almost a hand and feet climb over an outcrop of rock before I could get onto the level ground of the cave's mouth.

Inside I could see Mhairi standing, obviously having watched me approach. Bella ran up to greet her and they exchanged affection.

I said, 'Hello, it's Gareth.'

She mumbled something that sounded like, 'Yes I know.' Again the motif on her forehead stood out like a beacon and the weird headdress was still on her head.

'Is this where you live?' I asked.

She just nodded a reply. I could see I was going to have to work hard to get any real response on any subject. 'And in the winter?' I added. Again a nod in affirmation. 'Doesn't it get cold?' I pursued.

She pointed to the fire and a collection of fur skins at the back of the cave. There, in the distance I could also see a small aperture which obviously led further into the rock.

'It's quite dry in here and I get my water from down there,' she said pointing to the aperture. That was the first real sentence she had spoken to me. I found out later that she had to crawl in that aperture on her hands and knees for about thirty metres, then drop down about another forty metres to an underground pool to obtain her water. All this had to be undertaken in the dark, although she did have tapers to light.

'How did you find me?' she asked.

'I watched you walk this way when we parted on the mountain the other week. How long have you been living here?'

'I don't know exactly,' she replied. 'I was abandoned by my parents when I was very young and somehow found my way up here and I've lived here ever since.'

Again I found out later that her parents used to work a croft in one of the nearby woods, but when they couldn't make a go of it they just ran off and left her. Mhairi had never had any formal education. She couldn't read or write.

'But what do you live off. What do you eat?'

'I live off the herbs and plants all around here. There's also fish in the river. Do you want to try some herbs?' I nodded cautiously in confirmation. 'Jessie also sometimes gives me eggs,' she added.

I was offered a seat on one of the rugs behind which was a stack of cushions obviously made from animal skins and furs which acted as a bolster to enable me to sit up straight. She went to a jug and poured some liquid into a mug. 'Try that,' she said while handing it to me, then sat down on a similar perch alongside me. Bella sat between us. First I smelt the brew, which seemed sweet. Then I took a sip. It was like nectar and slid down my throat with little effort. I took a bigger gulp because of it's sweet strength, but then I nearly choked on it.

She laughed, for the first time. It made her look dramatically beautiful.

'Good?' she enquired.

'Very good,' I replied and continued to sip more delicately at the liquid.

Then as she had done with Jessie she broke into this gobbledegook of speech which I couldn't understand. Words like Macrinscarbles and skiddlelewadles, grimps and grarpes,' flew off her tongue like another language. Again later on I was to discover this was her way of expressing herself. Unlike the rest of us she had never been taught or learnt adjectives or any normal descriptive words. These phrases were her own compilations on matters of concern. While we were sitting there she even spoke to Bella in the same dialect.

I guess we sat like that for half an hour or more, chatting reasonably comfortably, whilst taking in the expansive view in front of us. From there I could see for miles across the valley and over the woodland where I worked. Most of her sentences were short and succinct. When she became animated about a subject the motif on her forehead glistened sparklingly and she gestured wildly with her hands and arms to emphasise her words when she wanted to make a point before breaking into the gibberish.

'You work for the forestry commission?' she asked me pointing at the woodland below.

'I do,' I responded, 'but I've only just started with them a week or so ago. It's the only work I could get around here.'

'You shouldn't cut down the trees,' she said starkly next.

'Well at the moment I don't actually do that. Up to date they only trust me with planting them.'

'Good. You mustn't cut them down. Trees are creatures, just like humans. When I'm in the wood I hear them talking to each other. They know when you are coming to cut them down. They tell each other. I hear them telling each other.'

Again she had taken me by surprise. I wasn't expecting such a comment to emit from her lips. 'I suppose though we do need timber to build things?' I volunteered in response.

'There are other materials,' she replied. 'Trees are precious.' There was no real reply I could make to that, but it did make me think.

After a while I could see that dusk was beginning to set in which meant Bella and I would need to make tracks for home before it got dark. If I could I wanted to cross the river in whatever daylight was left. Before we departed I said to Mhairi, 'How did you get that motif on your forehead?'

'I painted it on with herbs and flowers,' she replied.

'Can you remove it?' I asked.

'Not easily,' she responded. 'It covers a scar.' Again, much later on, I found out that the scar was inflicted by her parents hitting her with a shovel before they abandoned her. They left her for dead, but somehow Mhairi survived and brought herself up in these wild mountains.

The long walk back to my home gave me plenty of time to ponder on our meeting and what she had told me. There was no doubt that Mhairi was the most amazing person I had ever met in my life. The few words she had spoken to me which I could understand had put all my current problems into perspective. It had been impossible to guess her age, she could have been anything between twenty and forty and even she admitted she didn't know exactly how old she was, because she couldn't recall her age when her parents left her.

CHAPTER SIX

On the Monday morning I returned to work with a certain amount of new found vigour. I asked some of the old lags if they knew anything about Mhairi but all of them confessed that they had never seen her or even heard of her. From what she'd said to me though, she knew a lot about their activities in the forest. Apart from my work my most pressing problem at that time was what to do about the letter from my solicitor. Up until then I had deliberately ignored it but I realised I couldn't do that for much longer or the police might put out a warrant for my arrest. That was something I couldn't afford as it might prejudice my work situation in the highlands; my employers being a government organisation, and I was still on a six month probation period with them.

In the end I decided to write back to the solicitors stating that I rejected the accusations and didn't want to take time off from my new job. I thought at least the slow speed of mail back and fore to the highlands would string out the matter a bit longer. I had no telephone and of course all these events happened before the days of e-mails and mobile phones.

One evening on my after work walk with Bella I was in their work shed with Bob and Jessie when I mentioned my meeting with Mhairi. 'What did you know about her parents?' I asked them.

'They were a pair of rogues,' Bob replied. 'Constantly they were being arrested for poaching and the like. Sheep, fish, deer, they'd poach or rustle anything. Eventually because of the continual problems they were hounded out of the village. Somehow or another they managed to settle in a derelict croft in the forest up in the mountains, although they or their family never actually owned it. When they moved in as trespassers it was completely uninhabitable but they made it just about liveable. Out of sight was out of mind so nobody bothered about them much. Then one time they were involved in a big case of sheep rustling, so the law went after them again and that's when they absconded for good.'

'Did anybody know about Mhairi at that time?'

'No,' Jessie replied. 'She only appeared long after they had gone when she must have at least been a teenager.'

'So she must have survived by herself all that time,' I said.

'We presume so although we don't know for sure. Since then they've sent social workers and health people to try and contact her, but she doesn't want to know and somehow each time she manages to give all of them the slip. I think they've given up on it and leave her alone now.'

The more I learned about her the more fascinated I became.

* * * * *

Over those next few weeks I didn't see her again but in my work we changed our venue for planting. Early in the morning we were taken out to some new ground which entailed a boat trip across a loch. Bouncing about across the strong, wind induced waves in a twelve foot barge at seven thirty in the morning was another harrowing and mind-boggling experience. Usually there was a race among the lads to be the first aboard to get inside the small cabin and shelter from the wind. That day I had lost out in the scramble and had to endure the discomfort of the icy blasts on the open deck as we motored across. My perch in the foredeck did however enable me to witness the most marvellous spectacle. About a hundred yards in front of the boat I spotted a large herd of deer swimming across the loch. There must have been about thirty of them. The males were clearly visible with their antlers protruding out above the water. The others only displayed the top of their heads, the rest of their bodies were completely submerged. They were heading towards a small uninhabited island in the middle of the loch and moving at a fast pace. I pointed them out to one of the old lags and asked them about it.

'Och they are going over there for the day,' he said pointing at the island. 'In the daytime that's where they live as there are no people on the island. In the evening, when we have gone from the planting site they swim back to the mainland because there is fresh water and greener pasture to eat, plus our newly planted trees!' he guffawed. Their presence was a sight to behold and remained in my mind for a long time.

Sometime later in the week I received a letter from my solicitor which stated that the police back home definitely wanted to see me about Janet Lawrence's accusations. They confirmed that if I didn't respond they would issue a warrant for my apprehension. For many days I pondered on what to do. Eventually I decided that the best thing was to talk to my employers about it. I duly saw McIntosh and told him that there was a family problem back home that I needed to sort out. In a weeks time there was an up and coming bank holiday weekend, so I suggested that I travelled south over that weekend and be back a day or two afterwards. He agreed to that but added that as I was still on probation they would be unable to pay me for the lost working days. That cheered me up a lot.

I also had to make arrangements with Bob and Jessie to take care of Bella whilst I was away, so it was going to be a costly trip for me and no pay to cover it.

Then, one morning, early, before I left for work, I was shaving in my bathroom when Bella began to bark, which was unlike her unless something really disturbed her. My bathroom window opens out on to my rear small garden, where there are some shrubs and a deer fence. I opened the window to see if I could see anything. Dawn was breaking. In the gloom though I could just about make out the figure of Mhairi climbing out of my garden over the deer fence. I called out to her but in a trice she was gone, running away without any reply. Suddenly I realised that she had made an effort to find out where I lived. Maybe she is also interested in me as well I thought.

* * * * *

My trip south the following weekend was another arduous experience. I had made an appointment to be at my solicitors in Cardiff early on the Tuesday morning after the bank holiday break. They would then accompany me to the police station to meet up with the law.

Except for the odd foray to Fort William, for shopping, I had not been off the peninsular for three months and had forgotten what the outside world was really like. On the peninsular we have no roundabouts or traffic lights. No buses, except for a minibus to the ferry and not much traffic. To pass three cars on a journey is an exception.

Having deposited Bella and her food for the stay with Bob and Jessie I drove in my little beat-up van to the ferry. After crossing to the mainland I then caught the four o'clock bus to Glasgow which arrived there at ten o'clock in the night. Then the overnight train to Birmingham on which I tried to sleep, but achieved very little. There I had to wait three hours for the connecting train to South Wales. My ablutions and attempts to freshen myself up were completed in the railway station toilets. Fortunately my solicitors offices were situated in town so it only necessitated a short walk to their premises.

There I was met by Gwyn James, the partner who looked after my affairs. He was a tall man in his early fifties with a balding head, pince-nez glasses and wearing the customary dark suit. He greeted me cordially and offered me a coffee for which I was grateful.

'Well whatever your problems Gareth I have to say you look well. The outdoor life must suit you.' With all my problems I had forgotten how wind tanned my face had become. In comparison he looked pale, pasty, overweight and office bound.

'Ay it's a great life if you don't weaken,' I replied, mimicking a Scottish accent.

We discussed the sort of things the police might quiz me on. Up until then they still hadn't told us what their new evidence was, although James indicated that as far as he could gather there were some witnesses to events that might go against me. I confessed that I couldn't think of who or what that might entail for, as far as I was concerned, I had never accosted Janet Lawrence in any way. When the time came we headed for the police station, which was another short walk away. On the way there I couldn't get over the continual hum, noise and volume of the traffic, which I hadn't experienced for months. In a strange way it made me feel slightly dizzy.

At the police station we were led through to an inner, stuffy interview room where we were eventually joined by two gruff sounding detectives, who had obviously already made up their minds that I was guilty of whatever crimes I was accused of. Maybe it was because I wasn't wearing a suit and tie and as there is no barber in my highland village I had let my hair grow. It wasn't exactly a hippy style but it was certainly longer than it would have been when I worked in the newspaper office. I guess also that as I had escaped to live in the wilds of Scotland they had presumed that I had done so to evade prosecution on the accusations made against me.

From the outset they were offensive. They wanted me to confirm details of my employment at the newspaper and my relationship with Janet Lawrence. Then they quizzed me on why I had gone to live in Scotland. Obviously it was painful for me to recount the matters surrounding Anne's death and the resulting depression. Although Gwyn James tried to regularly intercede on my behalf, the two coppers remained belligerent towards me. Despite what James or I said I became more and more convinced that they had already made up their minds about the case against me.

Gwyn James did ask them what was the new evidence they had.

I was taken aback when they rolled out a list of sightings of me groping or physically handling Janet Lawrence. In response I rejected all the accusations and instantly asked them to name the people who had seen those events. They said that at this stage they were not allowed to do that. James tried pressing them on the issue but he got no further on it than me.

We finished up with them stating that they felt they had enough evidence to send the papers to the public prosecutor. There followed a long con-flab about how to get hold of me in Scotland. They couldn't understand or believe that I didn't have a telephone. They scoffed when I said there was a phone box about a mile up the road from my house which was perfectly suitable for my purposes when I needed it. They made copious notes about my address and couldn't understand that it didn't have a street name. They asked me where was the nearest police station. I advised them that it was about a mile down the road in the other direction from the phone box. They wanted to know about it. I told them it was manned by Jack Banyard who was the sole policeman on the peninsular and I stated that occasionally I shared a drink and a blether with him at the local hotel on Friday nights. They both sighed heavily. A smile crossed James's face. They asked if I would object if they contacted me through him. I wasn't really happy with that but I couldn't refuse. And that was it. They said that I would be hearing from them.

James walked back with me to the railway station. His feeling was that they would proceed with the case. I said I would keep in touch with him. Then there was nothing left for me to do but to grab some food at the railway station café and await the next train for Birmingham. Afterwards there was the long train journey to Glasgow, then I had to wait for the first bus at eight o'clock in the evening, which would arrive at Fort William at eight o'clock in the morning. All of that gave me plenty of time to brood on my problems but by the time I reached the ferry I was no closer to finding any answers.

My little van was waiting for me on the peninsular for the journey to my home. For once the sun was out and the one redeeming feature of the whole few days was to drive through the mountain pass to my cottage. After the noise and grime of the city, the hills looked bonny. As I drove one of the thoughts that went through my head was that I was never going to leave this place, whatever it took. At Bob and Jessie's I received a boisterous welcome from Bella and we were both able to enjoy our favourite forest walk.

* * * * *

The meeting with the police in South Wales had added to my worries and disillusionment. I felt that my back was now up against a brick wall with no possibility of escape. At home in the peace and serenity of my highland bungalow I made a valiant attempt to rationally put together the pieces of the jigsaw that had resulted in my being in that situation.

As I have described, in the months after Anne's death the real trauma began with Janet Lawrence's accusations. Up until then, in my own way, I had sort of coped with the bereavement of a loved one but Janet's actions were almost the final straw.

With the assistance of alcohol and being off work with nothing else to occupy my mind, I had pretty quickly descended into a morose state of morbid depression. I didn't want to go out, I didn't want to see any of my friends. When I did I was usually curt and offhand with them, so they gradually began to ignore me.

During those weeks the police came to see me at my home in Cardiff on three separate occasions about Janet Lawrence's accusations. That of course didn't help my state of mind either. When they'd gone I again resorted to heavy use of the whisky bottle and usually ended up crashing out asleep in a drunken stupor. On their last visit I got the impression that they hadn't been able to gather enough evidence against me to warrant any charges, although they didn't tell me that. When I hadn't heard from them for a fortnight I phoned them and they did more or less admit the same thing. Before slamming the phone down on them however, I did manage to spit out, 'Well why didn't you let me know.' Their reply was some non-committal mumbo jumbo.

Then I had the task of sorting the matter out with my employers. I duly telephoned Clifford Johns my editor who said he would have to check with the police and then speak with the directors about it. That took another three days before he came back to me, which dragged out more purgatory. When he did return my call what he told me sent me further down the spiral.

'The directors have decided that to avoid further problems between the two of you we can't have you working in the same building.'

There was a moments silence on the line so I broke it by saying, 'And?'

'We feel that it would be better if, for a time, you worked for our sister paper in Swansea.'

I needed to exert the utmost control to stop myself exploding down the phone to him but I withheld anything drastic as I guessed that my job was still on the line. 'Why am I the one who has to go Swansea?' I just about managed to spit out. 'I'm told that I have done nothing wrong. Why isn't she sent to work in Swansea.'

'Well Gareth that's the decision the directors and editors have come to. You can either take it or leave it. We will pay for your lodgings down there for three months to see how things work out.'

His words left me flabbergasted. 'And that's your final decision?' I just about managed to stutter out.

'I'm afraid Gareth that is the management's final decision. I will write to you outlining everything.'

After I had put the phone down I crumpled in a heap on the sofa and reached out onto the sideboard for a glass and the bottle of whisky. Because of the distance involved to Swansea and the awkward hours journalists have to work I knew that there was no way I could travel back and fore daily from home and would therefore have to take up his offer of staying there in digs. In the state of depression I was in I was convinced that was the last thing I needed. Needless to say I got myself into a right stew about it.

A couple of days later Clifford Johns' letter arrived spelling out the details of the arrangement, which added to my gloom. The newspaper wanted me to start work in Swansea on the first day of the following month. As he had said they would find and pay for my lodgings there and allow me mileage petrol allowance for one journey up and back to my home in Cardiff per week. I sat for an hour or more staring at the letter whilst consuming more whisky. Then I realised that I would have to get myself into some sort of mental and physical shape before recommencing work. I resorted to taking long walks around our neighbourhood in the gloom of the dark winter evenings.

* * * * *

My first day at the offices of our sister paper in Swansea was fractious and unpleasant. I got the feeling that my work colleagues there resented me coming onto their patch. They appeared to be a very close knit crew. For years there has also been a history of antagonism between the two cities, which has, to some extent, centred around the competition between the two respective football and rugby teams. The rivalry and one-upmanship in that respect is, and has, continued to be intense. It also very quickly became obvious to me that the editors there had given no consideration as to what role I might play in their set up. I soon realised that as far as they were concerned I was just a spare part that they didn't really know what to do with, so I was given the bum jobs. In addition I guess a certain amount of gossip relating to Janet Lawrence's accusations against me had filtered down the line and as usual most people assume that there is no smoke without fire, which didn't help my cause at all.

Retreating to my digs in the evening brought no relief. The accommodation was a typical one night stopover facility for sales reps. The dining room did overlook the Mumbles Bay, but my single room at the back was small dark and dingy with a window that provided no view, except for a blank brick wall. It was definitely no place to relax and unwind in. My only consolation was that the guest house fronted onto the Mumbles Bay and in the evening I was able to walk back and fore along the promenade, deep breathing and taking in the sea air.

By the end of the first week I'd almost had enough. To be able to retreat to the sanctity of my own home at the weekend was a godsend, but my spirits and health continued to get lower and lower. Reluctantly I had to force myself to return to my Swansea digs on the Sunday night. The only motivation to do that was the monthly mortgage payment I had to pay on my own home. As the weeks ticked by my state of health became worse, mainly due to the heavy drinking and the personal reaction towards me in work.

In amongst all of that I had to attend an inquiry into Anne's death at the hospital where it had occurred. The event was a complete nightmare for me. Although her family were also present I was reduced to the role of an outsider. They didn't blame me for anything but because of our single status I was not actually a member of their close family and therefore not really involved in their discussions. The inquiry decided that the hospital was negligent and a substantial sum of money was paid out in compensation. Needless to say, as I wasn't a relative of Anne and as she had made no Will, I received nothing. Her family's commiserations to me were parsimonious, which only added to my depression and disillusionment.

As a result again my drinking and depression increased and I was aware that my work was getting sloppy, for which I was duly chastised by the editors in Swansea. It became obvious to everybody, including me that I was not fitting into the working environment there. Matters came to a head when because of a succession of hangovers I started arriving late for work in the morning. I was reprimanded for this but relating my side of my troubles fell on deaf ears. It all came to a head when one day I was violently sick in the office, due to the effects of a lunch time drinking session and had to go back to the digs early. Next day I was given a letter by the editors pointing out all the warnings they had given me. I regret to say I couldn't recall half of them, but I'm sure they were right in what they were saying. At the end of the letter it was spelt out that they had no alternative but to give me a months notice to leave.

In a way I was half pleased but I knew it spelt disaster for me. I did telephone my office back in Cardiff but they said they couldn't take me back there due to Janet Lawrence's complaint. When I talked to the Swansea editors about it they confirmed that I wouldn't have to work out my notice if I didn't want to, but they did say they would honour their offer to pay me up until the end of the month for which I was grateful.

I can't say that packing up the few belongings I kept at the digs caused me any real heartache and as I drove along the M4 back to my home I was, in a way, quite relieved. The one sweet ounce of comfort when I got there was to be reunited with my familiar possessions and furniture. Reality set in though when I sat on my sofa and realised that at the end of the month I would be unemployed with no income and a hefty monthly mortgage to pay. The thought of signing on at the social security office was a recurring nightmare.

For a number of days I pondered on the best course of action for me to take. When I couldn't reach any satisfactory decision, on the spur of the moment, I decided to take myself away from there for a few days to try and clear my mind. I still had my car, and my pay for that month which would cover the petrol money for wherever I wanted to go. With the benefit of hindsight it was the best decision I ever made.

In my younger student days I had hiked and stayed at many Youth Hostels throughout the western highlands of Scotland. Thoughts of those wonderful carefree days, walking for miles in the cool fresh air, amongst some of the best mountain scenery in the world, inspired me to immediately seek out my walking boots and clothes, my old neglected knapsack and tacky waterproofs. In my untidy, under the stairs cupboard, amongst all that clobber I also discovered a tattered, well thumbed map of the region. I spent the rest of the evening studying it and planning a route.

Next morning I organised myself to set off before dawn. My aim was to pass Manchester before the morning work traffic got going. I calculated that if I drove non stop all day I should reach the highlands sometime before dark. My aim was achieved and I was able to sign in at a Youth Hostel in Glencoe by about six that evening. To step out of my car and taste the fresh mountain air was a blessed relief.

During those few days I climbed many Munro's (mountains over three thousand feet) and also took the ferry across Loch Linnhe to where I now live. Whilst driving along the narrow road that led to another peak, Ben Resipol, I spotted a 'To Let sign' on a roadside bungalow. I got out of the car, walked up to the front door and rapped my fist on it. The silence that greeted me told me there was no one inside so I walked around the outside of the property peering in through the windows. When I eventually returned to the front door and looked at the imposing view of the mountains in front of me I said to myself, 'this has to be the place.' A small stream babbling alongside the adjacent road added to the attraction of the bungalow's situation.

As soon as I was back home in South Wales the first thing I did was put my property there on the market for sale. At the end of the month I also had to endure the indignity of signing on the dole. I can't say they were pleasant days, but at least the activity of organising the house sale and the proposed letting in the highlands did give my brain the opportunity to work on something constructive. Although my property was mortgaged there would be a little bit of equity left after paying off the loan and I raised some other money from a garage sale of my furniture, which all in all would keep me going financially for a few months in Scotland. To my frustration the house sale took three months to complete. Gwyn James acted for me in all the transactions which helped particularly with the peculiarities of Scottish agents who were letting the property there. Finally I sold my car and purchased a small van that was big enough for me to transport my remaining possessions to the Highlands. As I drove north I can't say that I had any regrets about leaving my former home in South Wales, as the last year or so there had been the most trying period of my life.

CHAPTER SEVEN

Returning to the Highlands after my trip to Cardiff was a major relief. In a strange way the whole experience down south had shown me how lucky I was to live in such a beautiful remote place. Although the cloud of Janet Lawrence's accusations were still hanging over me I was more able to put the whole matter into perspective. Next day I was instantly reinvigorated with my work there and the comradeship of my working colleagues. Therefore in many respects I considered myself a fortunate man, although there were still days of depression brought on by past events.

The daily work remained tough and physical, especially as the winter weather was beginning to settle in. Freezing frosts were a regular feature, making a seven thirty start even more challenging. Sometimes the frosts prevailed all day, although it did make the mountain views even more spectacular with endless clear, cloud free skies. Because of the advent of the frosts as a squad we became less involved with planting and I was seconded onto a fencing project, which meant that the commission must have been reasonably pleased with my work. It also meant I could earn more money.

Then, one evening the strangest thing happened. I was settling down to watch TV with Bella curled up at my feet. I had a log fire going in the lounge when she barked and got up and made for the lounge door. I followed her out of the room towards the kitchen and the back door of the bungalow. There was the sound of rapping on it which is what must have disturbed her. I thought that was strange as I hardly ever got callers at that time of night. Bella was sniffing at the door and whimpering. I opened it with trepidation not knowing what to expect because on the rare occasions I got callers they usually came to the front door. What I saw outside amazed me. I had put the outside light on and standing under its glare was Mhairi, yet she looked completely different. She wasn't wearing her beret which revealed that she possessed the most gorgeous short black hair. On her face there was make-up but it wasn't anything like the make-up I had ever seen before. At a guess I would say it consisted of the products of flowers and herbs, but it made her face glow in a startling manner. The motif however still stood out on her forehead. She also wasn't wearing the type of clothes I had seen her in before. Her outside attire consisted of what looked like two or three different expensive duffle coats that had been sewn together to make one outer coat with a sheepskin collar. Bella jumped up at her and made a big fuss of her whilst I let her into the bungalow. I was too tongue tied and dumbfounded to say much. Mhairi then broke into her unintelligible dialect. There were lots of skidilywadles, machrinscarbles and mesemblenes. I was totally confused and completely gaga. I guided her through to the lounge. Bella followed whilst repeatedly jumping up at her.

Due to the heat from the fire the first thing she did was remove the duffle coat. 'It's hot in here,' were the first proper English words she said to me.

Underneath the coat she was wearing a dress which was obviously made from various different silks sewn together and ending just above her knees. It displayed an almost classic nubile figure. I took the coat from her, left the lounge door open and offered her a seat on the settee which she accepted, crossing her legs as she sat down to reveal large areas of bare thigh. She wore no shoes on her feet, I remained spellbound.

'It must be hot for you in here after your cave,' I said primarily because I couldn't think of anything else to say. 'Can I get you a drink? I have some wine?' she agreed and I went to the kitchen cupboard and took out the only bottle of cheap white sauvignon I had in the bungalow and two glasses. Bella stayed with her, exchanging affection.

Bella's head was resting on Mhairi's lap, occasionally receiving a stroke, as I poured out two glasses of the wine. I sat down next to her on the settee. 'It's nice to see you,' I said raising my glass in toast. 'I feel honoured that you should come to visit me.'

'You visited my home so I had to return the favour,' she said while raising her glass in a reciprocal toast. Instantly she coughed chokingly after the first sip just as I had done with her home made brew. We both laughed out loud. Again her face looked beautiful. There followed another bout of her unintelligible expletives expressing herself about the wine from which I couldn't tell if she liked it or not.

Gradually, although very slowly and deliberately, we began to talk to each other. Sometimes she didn't understand what I was saying and vice versa, but we got by. She admired the pictures on the walls, although they weren't up to much and pointed at the television and asked, 'What's that?' I had switched it off when she had entered the room, so I got up and switched it back on again. She laughed even more when the picture came alive. I showed her the different channels and how I switched them from one to the other. She admitted that she had never seen anything like it before and got up to touch the screen and peer into it. I let her play with the relevant channel buttons. She couldn't believe that she could switch it on and off repeatedly. She pointed at my record collection and again asked what those were. I took one out of it's sleeve and put it on the record player turntable to play. Again she couldn't believe it and pressed her head to the speakers.

I guess we must have continued conversing like that for an hour or so. By then it was reaching nine o'clock when she said, 'It's getting late I have to go now.'

I looked out the window at the darkness and the freezing cold and said 'you can't go back to your cave at this time of night, it's too dark and cold and you'll fall over and hurt yourself or catch pneumonia.'

'P'hh,' she puffed, then said, 'camanunhanish,' whatever that meant and continued with. 'I live in the mountains. I know every step. You should see how cold it gets here in the New Year.'

'I won't let you. I would never forgive myself if anything happened to you. You must stay here until the morning.'

She looked at me defiantly. For a moment I thought she was going to stalk out, but then she said, 'Ok I will sleep here' she said, pointing at the sofa.'

'Good I will get some blankets.'

'P'h,' she responded again. 'No blankets. It is too hot in here. I have my coat if it gets cold,' she said pointing at it.

So that was how it was left. We both made our separate arrangements for sleep, me in my bed and her on the sofa, with Bella in the kitchen. Before I put out my light I could hear her chanting again as I had heard and seen her do on the top of Sgurr Dhòmhnaill. I presumed that was her way of praying. I put my light out and eventually fell asleep.

Sometime in the early hours I was disturbed by a rustling in my room. At first I thought it was Bella, as sometimes in the night she would push my bedroom door open with her nose and come in. The next thing I knew I could feel this naked body getting into bed alongside me.

'I was lonely in there and couldn't sleep,' she said. 'I'm not used to sleeping in a room. I can't breathe.'

For a moment I thought I was having one of my stupid dreams. However this time when I turned over this gorgeous nubile body fell into my arms. For a while we held each other tightly. Then eventually my hands began to caress her curves. She responded likewise on my body and down to my vital parts. In due course I couldn't resist her any more and turned her over on her back and made love to her. It was the most glorious sex. Her continuous soft moaning indicated that she enjoyed it too. Afterwards we both fell asleep in each others arms.

When I awoke in the morning I could see it was still dark outside. I felt the sheet alongside me but there was nothing but an empty space where her body had been. I put on the bedside light. My clock told me it was just gone five o'clock. I got out of bed and called out, 'Mhairi', but there was no response. Quickly I looked around the other rooms but she was nowhere. Her clothes and coat had gone from the lounge. In the kitchen I found Bella sitting at the back door looking at it. 'She's gone has she?' I said to the dog.

In time I had to get myself ready for work, although that morning it wasn't an easy task. A part of me still wondered if it had all been another of my fantasy dreams, but when I came to make my bed I could still detect the perfume of her body on the sheets.

I have to admit that that day's work was a struggle. I still couldn't properly decide if the previous night was a dream or not. Afterwards I tried not to think about it too much although that proved difficult. My work was now very exacting as we were constructing a deer fence across a mountain ridge, which in some parts was two thousand feet up and we had to walk up there in the morning before we began. It also meant that when I wasn't working I was too exhausted to go far, particularly as far as Mhairi's cave. I just about managed to take Bella on her evening walk as far as Bob and Jessie's, but they told me they had not seen her recently either, but added that it was often like that as sometimes she got trapped up there by the weather. The more I learnt about her the more I marvelled.

One evening there was a rap on my front door. Bella barked. I jumped up out of my chair hoping it might be Mhairi. My heart sank however when I opened the door and saw standing outside in the lashing rain the tall figure of Jack Banyard, our local policeman. Instantly I knew what he was calling about.

'You'd better come in out of that Jack,' I said, referring to the rain.

'A'ch it's a dirty night all right,' he said and I ushered him to a seat in the dining area. He took off his cap and it dripped water onto the carpet. He was a lanky thin man with receding dark hair and a gaunt face that looked like a policeman who had spent too many harrowing days in previous locations and was glad to wind down in this quiet backwater until his retirement. I knew he was already building a bungalow in the village for that eventuality.

'I've had a call from the police in Cardiff,' he began. 'They tell me the public prosecutor down there is beginning to prepare a case against you. I had to confirm to them where you were living.'

'I thought you might be calling about that.' I said. 'First off Jack I want to tell you that I had nothing to do with whatever allegations this woman Janet Lawrence has raised against me. I give you my word on that. It's just a case of spiteful jealousy on her part.'

'Well that's nothing to do with me,' he replied. 'I'm only telling you as they contacted me about your whereabouts. I expect in due course, if they go ahead, you'll receive a summons. If you do it will be best to attend for a trial as I don't want to have the job of having to take you into custody.'

'I thank you for telling me that Jack. I appreciate it. I wouldn't want to cause you any trouble. That's the last thing I would want to do.'

'What made you want to move up here?' he then asked.

Briefly I told him about Anne's death and my following depression. He listened impassively.

'Have you settled down. Do you like it here?' he asked.

'I like it very much, especially now I have found work.'

'Ay it's not a bad place to be for a quiet life,' he responded. 'I'll leave you in peace then,' he added, got up, put on his hat and headed for the front door.

'You take care Gareth,' he said as he went outside into the continuous lashing rain.

'Oh dear,' I said to myself as I went back into the lounge to be greeted by Bella.

* * * * *

One day, on what must have been a Saturday as I wasn't in work, I was walking back from a shopping trip to the village, I hadn't taken Bella with me, when the most enormous storm erupted and the heavens opened. Heavy raindrops began to bounce high off the narrow single track road in front of me. Rather stupidly I hadn't taken an anorak with me and therefore had pulled my pullover over the top of my head to try and keep it dry. Then behind me I heard a car sloshing up the road. I looked around and stepped to the side to let it pass. I noticed that it was a dark blue Range Rover which I recognised as the vehicle of the wealthy McLeod family who lived across the valley from me. From my bungalow's front window I could see their large old estate type house nestled at the foot of one of the smaller mountains. The McLeods owned a lot of land in the area and from what I had learnt they also had substantial business interests away from the peninsular, although what type of business it was I didn't know.

Surprisingly the vehicle stopped and the passenger window rolled down. 'Can I save you from a soaking?' a woman's voice called out from inside. Then I was looking at a very glamorous well made-up face. Although she was wearing a baseball cap I could see that she possessed blonde hair which appeared to be tied up in a bun underneath. Occasionally I had seen her driving up and down the road but it was usually a view of the back of her head as she drove past me. This time however I had a full view of her very attractive face. In fact she was quite striking.

'That's very kind of you,' I responded a bit nervously. 'I'm afraid I'm soaked and will get your seats very wet.'

'Oh don't worry about that you won't make as much mess as the dogs do when they jump in here,' she replied, so I got on board, placed my shopping bag at my feet and pulled my jumper down from the top of my head.

'You're living in the Oliver's old bungalow?' She said in a very cultured voice, the accent of which certainly wasn't local, as we drove off.

'That's right,' I replied. 'How do you know that?'

'Oh you can't keep anything secret for long around here, everybody knows everything there is to know about everybody else. Don't worry though, you'll soon get used to it.' She was driving much faster than I would have done along that lane. 'Have you found some work?'

I explained that I had and was currently involved in a fencing project with the commission.

'That's good,' she said. 'That type of work is always needed around here with all the land and crofts.' As I got used to her presence I made a guess that she would have been in her mid thirties.

'Hey you've missed your turning I called out as we passed the narrow lane that led to her big house. To get the dwelling you had to cross a bridge over the small burn that runs past the front of my bungalow.

'I'll take you to your front gate,' she said. 'As I've said we can't have you getting soaked.'

As she drove on she asked where I'd come from and what I did down there. 'Well that's a bit of a change from here,' she said when I told her. Soon we were at my front gate. I thanked her profusely and made to get out of the Range Rover. 'I hope I'll see you again,' she said then added that her name was Carol.

'Me too, I'm Gareth,' I responded and stood by my front gate and watched her turn the Rover round with a swish and squeal of tyres. I waved as she sped off down the road. It was still raining cats and dogs but somehow I didn't notice it.

Throughout that weekend I couldn't get the thought of this woman out of my mind. Whenever I pictured her face I felt a stirring in my loins. I knew I shouldn't be thinking like that as I was aware she was married and had two young children. Fortunately work and a frosty early morning start on the Monday morning quickly banished such thoughts from my head. We were now well into the fencing project and were getting higher and higher up the mountain each day, which meant it was further to walk to start work and further back down when we finished. Although I was regularly exhausted I was still enjoying it.

What I feared most arrived during that week. In amongst my mail there was a letter from the public prosecutor in South Wales advising me to attend for a trial over the allegations Janet Lawrence had made against me. Fortunately the date indicated it was some two months away so it did give me time to think, although the first thing I did was write to Gwyn James my solicitor advising him of the situation and asking him to act for me in that instance.

His reply was back to me within a few days. He did however point out that it would be necessary to meet up with him and a barrister some time before the trial took place. More expense I could ill afford I thought.

Then another surprise occurred. I was coming out of the village store one day after work when Carol McLeod's Range Rover swept into the store's car park. When she alighted from the driver's seat she smiled delightfully and waved at me. The first thing I noticed as she got out of the vehicle were her long slim legs. She was wearing quite a short skirt and she was making sure I noticed everything on display.

You didn't see too many sights like that in the western highlands particularly in winter. For a few moments it took my breath away.

'Hello Gareth,' she said while continuing to walk towards me. The smile remained on her face and there was a slight tossing of the head to shake out the blonde hair, which that day extended down and over her shoulders.

'Hello, nice to see you,' I responded, trying to keep my voice steady.

'I've been hoping I might bump into you,' she began. 'We need some fencing work doing at the top end of our estate and I was wondering if you would be available for that. Obviously we would pay you the going rate for the job.'

I was flabbergasted. 'Of course I would,' I managed to stutter out. 'But it would have to be at the weekend because of my work commitments with the forestry.'

'I realise that. Perhaps you could pop over on Saturday and meet up with Angus to see what's involved.'

I agreed to that and arranged to call at their house at ten in the morning on that day. She then strutted off into the shop and I walked back to my bungalow with a spring in my step. Extra cash was something I badly needed, with an up and coming trip to South Wales and a court case looming over me.

CHAPTER EIGHT

On that Saturday morning I washed my hair, took a shower and put on the least awful set of working clothes I could find in my wardrobe. Most of my stuff was getting pretty threadbare; I hadn't done a proper shopping trip for those sort of items in months. Then I made the short journey over to the McLeod's dwelling in my van.

Close up the big old house was impressive. It was constructed in solid highland stone bricks with ivy covering some of the walls. At a rough guess I would say it was built in the early part of the twentieth century. I parked my van in as unobtrusive spot as possible and made my way to the big oak back door. There was a door knocker, which I attempted to use as politely as I could. The vocal retort of large dogs barking echoed inside in response.

In a matter of moments the door creaked open. I was greeted by Carol who was wearing a tight fitting red sweater, skin tight blue jeans, bare feet with her blonde hair hanging long. It all looked pretty intimidating.

'Ah, good, there you are, we've just finished breakfast,' she said while displaying a delicious smile. The barking had momentarily stopped. Behind her stood four red setters, panting. 'Angus has just gone to deal with the mail but I can offer you a cup a coffee while you wait and I clear away the breakfast. I'm afraid the place is in a bit of a mess.'

As I entered the hallway I was set upon by the hounds jumping all over me, fortunately in a friendly way. 'Get down you lot' she bellowed at them. 'Just ignore them Gareth, they're all stupid,' she said as I followed her down the passageway. I have to admit that it was pretty hard to ignore them but I kept moving.

She led me into the kitchen which wasn't a mess at all. In fact it was spacious and like something out of a kitchen designers magazine. She poured me coffee from a percolator and then set about clearing the breakfast dishes into the dishwasher. I found the sight of her bending over the machine quite stimulating while we talked about the weather.

Within a few minutes, Angus, a tall, big bluff Scotsman strode into the room. He possessed semi-grey hair and the strides of a giant. He called out my name and moved across the room to greet me with an iron fisted handshake. 'At least it's not raining,' he ventured. He was obviously at least ten years older than Carol.

'Ay,' I responded, attempting the local vernacular.

'Shall we go and take a look at the site?' I agreed and he began to put on his outside boots. He added, 'It will be quicker to walk. We could take the Rover but it will mean opening about six gates.' Again I agreed.

As he was putting on his wet coat two young children about aged six and eight charged into the room. The little girl who was the youngest was the spitting image of her mother, whilst the young boy was a mini version of his father.

'This is Rachel and Cameron,' Carol said. In reply I said hello but they both just giggled at me.

Soon Angus and I were outside, heading across the fields for the land at the foot of the hillside. On the way he asked me how I was settling down in the area and where and what I had done before. I replied with much the same answers as I had given Carol. It was a good puff up to the fence and on the way we had to climb over a few five bar gates. It was obvious though that Angus was a fit man. When we reached the fencing line you could see the problem. Clearly it was old, rusty and in many places collapsed.

'I've tried patching it up in places,' he began, 'but the sheep keep pushing it over. Then they get out and I have to go and look for them on the mountainside, so I have decided to replace all of it. Should have been done years ago, but it's one of those jobs you just don't get round to.'

We were by then walking along the fence's length. Do you want Rylock?' I asked.

'No, I don't really need to keep deer out I just want to keep the sheep in.' I was glad about that as Rylock, which is what I put up for the forestry, is really a two man job.

'I'll get all the wire, posts and nails in, so all you have to do is walk up here with your gear,' Angus said.

'It'll take a few weekends to do it all,' I responded.

'I realise that, but I'll pay you for each weekend as we go.' He then quoted me a price for each weekends work which was more than generous. As we walked back along the line we both paced out the distance and counted the number of posts, stobs and turners required. Angus had brought with him a notepad on which he wrote down all the requirements.

In time we were back in the house kitchen with Carol and the children. Carol continued to smile delightfully at me as we talked.

'If I can get all the materials in during the week, could you start next weekend?' Angus asked. I replied that I would be delighted to. He promised to let me know. After some more pleasantries I left them and drove away in my van feeling better than I had done in a long time.

For the first time since I'd been living in the Western Highlands my life began to take on a different aspect, although I still had the cloud of the forthcoming trial hanging over me. In all that time I didn't see Mhairi once. In the evenings, after work, because I was so tired, I got no further than Bob and Jessie's. They hadn't seen her for some time either and now I was going to be working weekends as well I just didn't have the time or energy to go climbing in the mountains to get to her cave. Her absence did worry me though, especially after our night of passion. I hoped she was all right.

Then later in the week I received another surprise. I had just returned from work and was about to attend to Bella when I heard a rapping on my front door. At first I thought it might be Jack Banyard with something to do with the summons, but I got a big surprise when I opened the door and saw Carol standing outside with a flashing smile on her face. She was wearing an expensive sheepskin coat.

'I thought I saw the forestry Land Rovers going down the road and hoped I might catch you in,' she said, then there followed a brief silence between us. I realised I had to invite her inside.

'Please come in,' I said. 'I'm afraid it's all a bit of a mess, I only have time to tidy and clean up at the weekends.' Fortunately I had shut Bella in the kitchen.

I followed behind her and noticed her look around the living room. 'It's not a mess at all,' she said. 'You should see the mess Angus and the children leave around our place when I go away for a few days.'

'I haven't had time to change,' I indicated by pointing at the state of my muddy working clothes.

'No worries. I think they make you look very rugged and attractive.' I was stunned into more silence. She continued by saying, 'I just came to tell you that Angus has got all the fencing materials and is wondering if you can start work at the weekend.'

I agreed that I could and we discussed the likely weather for those two days. Then she said she had to go and pick the children up from school. In a few moments she was gone leaving me with only the lingering smell of her perfume in the living room.

There was no lie-in for me on the Saturday morning. I was up at the same time as on a work day as I had to take Bella out before driving over to the McLeod's place. I was parking my van near their back door when Angus came out to greet me. 'I'll come up there with you to begin with,' he said. 'Just to check the stuff over and help you lay it out.'

We walked up the hillside together. He had with him the papers relating to the deliveries, while I carried my fencing equipment. Together we checked the stock then laid it out along the length of the fencing line. He was with me about an hour, then said, 'I'll leave it to you now.' Then he was gone.

My first job was to drive the posts and turners into the ground at regular intervals. This was the hardest part as you firstly had to dig a hole then drive the post properly into the ground with what is called a dropper and then a mallet. It was however easier than putting up Rylock as the posts weren't so high. Soon I was breaking into a sweat and needed to disrobe my wet jacket. Fortunately it wasn't raining, although the clouds out to the west looked ominous, so I cracked on.

At about midday I decided to stop and eat my piece. I didn't want to take long with that as the gloomy clouds looked to be getting closer. Then while I was sitting there I suddenly saw Carol McLeod coming up the fields and clambering over the gates towards me. 'Oh dear,' I thought.

When she was near she smiled and called out 'Hi Gareth, how are you getting on?'

'Ok,' I said. 'I've stopped for five minutes to eat,' I continued holding up my sandwich for her to see, 'but I don't want to be stopping long as the rain's coming.'

'I don't want you to stop for me,' she replied. 'As long as you're happy to chat while you work, if not I'll go away and leave you in peace.'

'No chatting is fine,' I responded and began to reaffix my fencing belt which contained all the nails and metal ties.

Soon I was back at work. She sat on the grass nearby and we talked. She wanted to know my reasons for moving to the highlands. I just told her I was fed up with my work down there and needed a change. I didn't mention any of the other problems. I discovered that she was from London and met Angus at a business function down there.

'Living up here, don't you miss the bright lights?' I asked.

'Sometimes but when I get itchy feet I go back there for a week or so. We have an apartment in the city.' Then I realised how wealthy Angus must be. 'But the quality of life up here is so much better especially for the children.'

We talked like that while I worked, then eventually she said, 'I must go down and make my family's lunch now. You seem to be doing very well.'

'Thanks,' I said, then she was gone.

I cracked on. By three o'clock the rain was quite heavy so I decided to pack up for the day. When I reached my van the back door opened and Angus stuck his head out. 'Time to pack up,' he said pointing to the sky and the rain.

'Ay,' I replied. 'Weather permitting I'll be back tomorrow.'

He waved and closed the door and I started up the van, heading for home and a hot shower.

The Sunday morning looked reasonably free of rain, for a while anyway, so early on I made my way across to the McLeod's place in my van. That morning there was no-one to greet me. The house seemed quiet and I guessed they were all still in bed. I therefore made my way up to the fence line as quietly as I could. Thankfully what I had erected on the previous day still remained in tact. Sometimes over night the deer will come down from the mountains to take a look at what you have been doing. Often they will butt against the newly erected posts to test if any are loose and try and loosen them some more. Then when the whole fence line is completed they will remember which posts they've loosened, butt them some more and barge through. I think they do this mainly out of a sense of cussedness, as if to say, 'That's not going to keep us out.'

However, on that day everything was Ok. I pressed on with the job as the approaching clouds in the distance looked ominous. Then as on the previous day, just before noon, I spotted Carol McLeod coming up the fields towards me.

'As it's cold I brought you some fresh coffee,' she said holding out a thermos flask towards me.

'That's very kind of you,' I replied. 'You didn't have to. You get used to the cold working in the forest and with this work you pretty soon get warm, but thank you.'

I stopped working and unscrewed the flask, then poured some into the cup top.

'You must be very strong to do all this by yourself,' she said next.

'Well I wasn't when I first started working with the commission, but you soon build up the muscles when you do this every day of the week.' I said whilst supping on the coffee. It was far better than any coffee I had at home and I guess it had come from the percolator.

'And very brave to come all the way up here to do it by yourself.'

I said nothing in reply and continued to sip. Then while I got back to work we continued to talk. In between I would stop to take more sips of coffee until I finished the flask.

'Very good, thank you,' I said after supping the last drop.

Again for about half an hour we talked, this time in a more relaxed manner than the previous day. She wanted to know more about my life in South Wales and eventually the question came up about if I had a wife or a girlfriend down there. I thought carefully before answering.

'I did have a girlfriend and we were going to get married, but unfortunately she died whilst having an operation in hospital.'

'That's awful. How long ago was that?' Carol responded.

'Oh about a year ago now.'

'Was that why you came to live up here?'

'Partly, but as I mentioned before there were some work problems as well.'

'Poor you. Well if you ever want to talk about it please don't hesitate to call me. I have some idea what it's like because I lost my mother when I was very young. I'm afraid I never completely got over that.'

We talked a little more, then she said, 'I'd better go.' She picked up the thermos flask and began to walk away. Before she'd gone very far she stopped and turned to face me and said. 'Now don't forget what I have said about calling me.'

'I won't and thanks,' I replied, then she was gone.

During all that period of time I never saw Mhairi and neither had Bob or Jessie. I was beginning to get worried. I still hadn't seen her since our night of passion. Because of my work and the fencing that I was doing for the McLeod's at the weekend I didn't have the time or the energy to go clambering up to her cave dwelling. Then, one day when I was working up the mountain on the Forestry fence line I thought I saw something move in the woodland a few hundred feet below us. It could have been an animal but I had a funny feeling it may have been her. I stopped and looked for some moments but I soon had to look away as the other lads were chastising me because they were holding onto the end of the Rylock waiting for me to attach it to the fence post. For the rest of the day though I thought about the sighting and wondered.

CHAPTER NINE

As the days passed the date of my forthcoming trial grew closer and I began to worry again. I continued to work on the McLeod's fence line at weekends. Carol was a regular visitor to the site and one day Angus accompanied her. I was by then almost three-quarters of the way through with the job and he seemed to be pleased with my work, although no real Scot is ever over enthusiastic with praise, but I had got used to that working with the other men in the Commission. With the extra work, for a time, I had been able to block the trial out of my mind, but suddenly it was looming in front of me.

I had been in touch with Gwyn James by correspondence to bring me up to date on the requirements and procedure. This time it would necessitate taking more than two days off work as I had to meet up with the Barrister before the trial. I therefore badly needed the extra money Angus was paying me as my stay down south would entail a nights stay in a hotel. Gwyn James in his correspondence had said that if all the charges against me were proved I could be facing a jail sentence, which cheered me up no end.

As before I had to make the same arrangements with Bob and Jessie for Bella and embark on the same car, bus and train journey. It was all very tedious and boring which gave my mind overtime to work on the problems that lay ahead of me. I hadn't mentioned to anybody up north the real reason for my trip south. In work I had to tell McIntosh that the same family problem had re-occurred and that I needed to go down there to sort it out, which I'd also told Bob and Jessie. I'd mentioned nothing at all about my journey to the McLeods as I hoped to be back by the weekend to finish off their fencing project. From what my solicitor had said though I might immediately be sent to jail, which would scupper everything. When I eventually arrived at the hotel in Cardiff I crashed out on the bed and fell into an exhausted sleep.

Later next morning I was due to meet up with the barrister. Firstly I called in on Gwyn James who was to accompany me to the barrister's chambers. He briefed me on what I could expect and the type of things the barrister would want to know. He was a man called Tom Bradley who was a tall overbearing man, who looked down at me from his great height as he spoke, whilst walking in continuous circles around the room.

Some of the questions and statements he threw at me quite shocked me. I knew this was a purported sex crime but some of the things he said or asked me were quite personal and I thought a bit over the top. For instance he asked that as my girlfriend had died was I getting sex anywhere else. However he later stated that these were the sort of things the prosecutor was likely to throw at me and he was only preparing me for that. He did also however go over with me my answers and suggested what I perhaps should respond with. In all I guess our meeting lasted about two hours and again I was quite mentally exhausted at the end of it.

When we all parted, with an agreement to meet up half an hour before the trial next morning at the court, I was left alone by myself wondering what the hell I was going to do for the rest of the day in the big city. Firstly I searched around for the cheapest self-service restaurant I could find for some lunch. Afterwards I did think about calling into my old newspaper office to see some of the lads, but immediately dismissed the idea when I realised I might run into Janet. So I did a bit of sightseeing around the city and again realised how noisy and traffic dominated the place was, even though many of streets were by then pedestrianised. In desperation I eventually found a cinema which was open and watched a film the title of which I can't remember nor very little of the plot. Most of the time my head was going round and round with what had been discussed at the barrister's office. Afterwards there was little else for me to do but watch the television in my hotel room. That night I slept very little as everything continued to spin in circles around my brain.

In the morning when I got up I was very confused and slightly disorientated. For a while I couldn't get my bearings and wondered where the heck I was. Drawing back the bedroom curtains to reveal a dull, uninspiring outlook soon brought the reality of everything in a city into life. Somehow I made it downstairs to breakfast but could only manage a couple of pieces of toast and a few cups of coffee. Then there was nothing more to do than wait in my room watching television until the clock ticked round to nine thirty when I made my way to the court room.

Fortunately, there I received a warm welcome from James and Bradley.

'We'll soon have you out of here,' Bradley said. 'Just try and remember the things we talked about yesterday.' Then we were eventually called into the court room.

Looking back on it all now I consider my trial was a complete fiasco.

Firstly the crown prosecutor was every bit as vicious and uncompromising about me in his descriptions of my activities, and his leading of his so called witnesses to castigate me in the same manner was as bad as my barrister had predicted. Fortunately as they continued their mendacity I was able to point out to my barrister the errors in their testimony. One of Janet's witnesses who was called did not even work in the same part of the newspaper building as us, so how she could have seen the things she described I had done I don't know. Another of the prosecution's witnesses I distinctly remember was away from the office, on a course, at the time of Janet's allegations. Thankfully with this information Bradley was able to tear their evidence to pieces. Looking across I could see that the jury didn't buy their pack of lies either. When Janet herself took the witness stand I nearly fell about laughing at the things she said.

'Gareth used to chase me around the office all day,' was one of her classic statements.

Beforehand I had already told my barrister about her advances towards me after Anne's death and emphasised that I had concluded that this trial was her way of getting back at me for my rejection of her. While she rambled on he continued to make her look a fool. Again I think the jury could see it was all a prefabricated story.

When it became my turn to take the stand the prosecutor continued with his character assassination of me about me getting sacked from my job and my disappearance to the western highlands of Scotland, but I was able to counter it all by recalling that Janet's accusations were made at a time I was still in mourning after Anne's death and that I had in fact rejected her advances as I had no wish or desire to engage with another female at that time. While I spoke these words I again looked across at the jury and they seemed to take in what I said. After my time on the stand the judge gave a brief summing up where he appeared to indicate that there was no case for me to answer to. We all retired to the waiting room to await the jury's decision.

'I don't think they've got a leg to stand on,' my barrister said. 'And anyway we will appeal if the verdict goes against us,' he added.

The jury were not out long. They returned a unanimous verdict of not guilty. The judge dismissed the case and I was awarded costs to cover my legal fees and my journey south and the hotel expenses. As a result I felt justified in indulging in another nights stay at the hotel before embarking on the long journey home. Compared to my life in the highlands the accommodation provided was positively luxurious although it was only a two star hotel.

Next morning I had to gird myself up for the trek north, although this time my body and mind felt more relaxed and I was able to peacefully doze on many parts of the lengthy train section. I made sure though that I was wide awake to take in the scenery through Crianlarich, Tyndrum, Rannoch Moor and the mountains of the Ben Nevis range. None of them had lost their grandeur and magnificence during my absence. To be reunited with my little van on the other side of the ferry crossing at Ardgour was like meeting up again with an old friend. As I drove towards my home, through the mountainous glen, the same thoughts passed through my head as before, in that I never wanted to leave this place again. I received a boisterous welcome from Bella at Bob and Jessie's residence. Compared to the inhabitants of Cardiff, Glasgow and Birmingham I had been rubbing shoulders with over the previous few days they both appeared to be from another world, another time and a different planet. I doubted that either of them had ever been in a big city store in all their lives. They still hadn't seen or heard anything of Mhairi.

When I walked in through the front door of my bungalow I hadn't realised until then how sparse it was without heat and light. I needed to prepare myself a meal and organise myself for work next day. At the weekend on the Saturday I also had to take myself off to the McLeod's place. The job there was nearly done. Just a few fill-in bits and tidying up to complete. Later in the morning I spotted Carol approaching with the familiar flask of coffee in her hand.

'Have you been away this week?' she asked when she was near. 'I didn't see a light on in your bungalow for a couple of nights.'

'I had to go down south to sort out a family matter,' I replied. We left it at that. 'I should be finished up here today,' I added.

'Oh well if you call in the house on your way past I'll organise for Angus to pay you, he's here this afternoon.'

After some more conversation about my trip south she made her way back to the big house.

I was able to finish up on the fence line that afternoon. As I was loading up my van outside their house, both Angus and Carol came out to see me.

'You've done a good job up there,' he said pointing up to the fence line.

'I've added a bit more cash as a bonus.'

'I'm most grateful,' I responded. Carol had a gushing smile on her face.

'I'm sure there will be more work like that available soon,' Angus said, 'if you're up for it?'

'Certainly will be,' I replied.

With that I got in my van and drove away to their accompanying waves and smiles.

CHAPTER TEN

I was soon back into the work and the craic with the fencing squad in the mountains. Knowing that the trial and all its implications were behind me lifted a great weight off my shoulders. I felt more relaxed and carefree in everything I did and for the first time started to really enjoy the ambiance and the lifestyle of the highlands. I began to socialise more and even participated in some of the local events.

I still hadn't seen or heard anything about Mhairi though and neither had Bob or Jessie. I became very worried about her and wondered if she was ill or perhaps had fallen badly and couldn't walk. Anything could happen to her up there in her isolated mountain abode and nobody would know anything about it. So, as I had by then finished the weekends fencing job at the McLeod's place, one Sunday I decided to trek up into the mountains with Bella and make for the cave. It was a warm day and I had forgotten how far and how long it took to get there.

When the cave's entrance came into view I was worried further as I could really see no activity around the place. Previously, when I had visited, I had seen smoke from her open fire. This time there was nothing. With every stride I became more worried and quickened my pace.

As I scrambled up the rocky outcrop to the entrance I called out her name but received no response. With one final heave I lifted myself up and over the outcrop of rocks and into the cave proper. There at the far end I saw Mhairi engaged in a twirling hypnotic dance whilst singing and humming to herself. Bella barked and ran towards her. She had obviously not heard us as we had approached. I called out her name again, this time even louder.

Our appearance obviously shocked her, for she turned around and gave me a startled stare. 'Gareth! Bella!' she shouted out and they became involved in another affectionate tangle. 'What are you two doing here?'

'We've come to see you, silly. What do you think we're doing here? Are you all right. Nobody has heard from you for weeks?'

For a few moments she hesitated with her reply. That gave me time to look at her properly. Her facial and physical appearance seemed to have changed. In those few moments I couldn't put my finger on it but she definitely looked different. If anything I thought she'd put on weight.

'Of course I'm fine,' she eventually responded, then went into a spasm of her gobbledegook language before twirling and humming to herself again. Bella jumped up at her and joined in with the dance. 'I've been having my musical period,' she said when she stopped. She then poured us both a drink from her liquid brew and some water for Bella, then pointed to her reclining pillows and cushions for us to sit on. Bella sat on the other side from me licking Mhairi's arm. I again spluttered after my first sip on the drink. We both laughed. 'It's nice to see you again,' she said as she toasted me with her cup. I responded likewise. She said that she knew I had been away and wanted to know where I had been. I didn't know how she knew that but I told her that I'd been back home, down south, to sort out a family matter. Perhaps she had been keeping a check on my house, I thought. The more we talked and relaxed in each others company the more I could see that her face definitely looked more rounded.

It was when she got up to get us both another drink that I noticed something else. When she bent down to reach for the pot that the liquid was contained in, part of the loose clothes around her midriff became slightly undone. Then I could see the bump protruding from her stomach. Even I knew enough to know that was not excess fat. That was a pregnancy bump.

'What's that?' I asked pointing to the protruding lump as she sat down beside me and handed me my drink. She began by mumbling some more ishgedoius and skiddlewadles. I wasn't going to be put off though and said abruptly, 'Mhairi are you pregnant?'

'Don't be so stupid, Raspunken,' she responded icily and added some more of the gobbledegook.

'Mhairi have you seen a doctor? If what I am thinking is correct, you must see a doctor.'

'I don't go in for doctors up here,' she said. 'I've never used one in the past why do I need to use one now?'

'You need to use one now because if what I think is correct you have more than just yourself to worry about now. There's another human being inside you now!'

'P'h,' she exclaimed and went into another tirade in her own mumbo jumbo.

We continued to argue about it until we left. I guess you could say that was our first proper argument and I discovered that she was a difficult woman to argue with. I trumped back down the mountainside cursing and swearing to myself and Bella about Mhairi's stupidity, whilst regularly tripping over protruding rocks and loose stones. Bella also kept getting in my way which didn't help matters or my temper.

Throughout the early part of the following week I continued to worry about the ramifications of what I had observed on Sunday. If what I thought was correct I could be the father of her unborn child. On one of my after work walks with Bella I mentioned to Bob and Jessie what I had spotted on my Sunday excursion to Mhairi's cave.

'From what you describe you could be correct,' Jessie replied. 'If I saw her myself I could pretty much tell if you were right or not, but she hasn't been near us for weeks now. Like you, we were beginning to worry.'

'Perhaps she has found herself a man up there,' Bob said. 'Although I don't know who else would want to go up there where you describe. They'd have to be more or less as nuts as she is to want to go up there,' he added.

I made no comment in response to that but I did notice Jessie's long hard stare at me. 'If she is in that condition she needs to see a doctor,' I did say though. 'I tried telling her that but she wouldn't listen to me.'

'I don't think she listens to anybody,' Bob responded. 'That's the trouble with her.'

During the week, on my way around the village store for my groceries, I bumped into the local District Nurse, who I had met a couple of times for the minor injuries I had suffered with my work for the Commission. I explained the situation I had seen with Mhairi and my concern about her getting medical attention.

'Oh we've all given up on her,' she responded impatiently. 'Long before you came here, the Forestry Commission even took the doctor up to that cave of hers in their helicopter, but she didn't want to know. As I said we've all given up on her. If she wants to come down and see us we'll attend to her, but we're not traipsing up and down the mountain again and getting no thanks for it.'

All week I worried about the situation, for if my hunch was correct, I was the one who was responsible for Mhairi's condition. Again it was something I could not offload onto somebody else as I had already discovered, which made it harder to live with. I therefore decided that I would have to go up the mountain again on the Saturday morning and confront Mhairi with the reality of it all.

That morning the weather was not good. There was rain about which made the crossing of the swollen river difficult. A couple of times I nearly toppled over and in the process got my trousers soaking wet. As a result the rest of my walk up to the cave was made even more unpleasant by the cold wind whipping through the damp material. My mood therefore wasn't good when I climbed over the rocky outcrop and into the cave.

This time there was no sign of Mhairi. I called out her name and Bella sniffed around the cave searching for her scent but we both got nowhere in that respect. I stood next to the fire which was flickering away in its home made hearth and attempted to dry out my trousers. It was a good ten minutes before, like Houdini, Mhairi eventually appeared out of nowhere from the back of the cave. Bella ran towards her and jumped up at her affectionately.

'There you are,' I began rather abruptly.

'Yes, here I am,' she replied in an equally exasperated manner.

'I've been waiting here for about ten minutes.'

'Well I'm sorry about that,' she responded in the same manner. 'I wasn't expecting you. I've been down in the lower cave collecting water. It's easier to do that when it's been raining as the water level is higher and it's easier to reach.'

'How are you?' I asked trying to hold onto my patience.

'As you see I am fine. Gareth I don't expect you to keep visiting me like this,' she said.

'Well in a way I feel partly responsible for your condition.'

'Oh what condition is that?'

'You know quite well that I think you are pregnant.'

'And you're an expert in these matters are you?' she responded.

'No, but I can see what I would consider to be evidence of that. And if that is the case I feel partly responsible.'

'Why do you feel responsible?'

'Because we spent the night together and had sex.'

'Gareth, you do assume an awful lot. If that's how you're going to be I don't think I want to see you again.'

'I've come to see you because I care about you,' I retorted abruptly.

'Well that's very nice but I've managed by myself before I met you and I'm quite capable of managing by myself now. That's how you become when you live alone like I do. Other people don't come into the picture at all. Each day I have to get on with whatever presents itself. I've never known anything different.'

'Would you prefer me not to visit you?' I asked.

'Perhaps that might be the best.' she replied.

We stood in silence and looked at each other for some moments. 'Well if that's what you want that's what I'll do,' I said. 'But if you need to see the doctor I will take you there.'

She nodded her head in response but didn't say anything.

'Come on Bella,' I called out as I turned and headed for the cave's opening. At first the dog didn't respond and remained standing alongside Mhairi. When I called a second time Bella licked Mhairi's hand then came after me. Our scramble down the mountain was tortuous and unpleasant. The rain had increased, the wind had got up more and I cursed and swore most of the way and I got another soaking when we crossed the river.

CHAPTER ELEVEN

'FIRE' is a word that is most dreaded and not repeated amongst forestry people. It's a word that is only used in exceptional circumstances when it actually happens. My introduction into the hazards of that trauma happened one clear, windy night. The weather had been dry for a couple days beforehand and a gusty wind added to the chaos and drama of the proceedings.

It began at about one thirty in the morning with the sound of somebody hammering on my front door, which sent Bella into a cacophony of barking. I struggled to put on my dressing gown and tripped over my slippers in my haste to reach the direction of the noise. Bella was out of her bed and reached the door before I did.

Outside, with the wind blowing through his tousled hair, stood McIntosh. 'We've got a blaze going well in the Ahern valley,' he said. I was too stunned to make a response. 'Get your gear on and I'll be back for you in ten minutes,' he added, and said he was going to pick up some of the other lads.

As fast as I could I donned my working clothes, poured out half of Bella's breakfast into her dish and topped up her water bowl. That at least kept her quiet while I put on my boots. I think she must have thought it was her birthday having her breakfast that early. I was walking down my driveway as McIntosh's Range Rover pulled up outside my front gate. It was a clear night with a moon up.

There were four other lads from the village in the Rover. I clambered into the back. 'Well done Gareth,' McIntosh said. 'There's quite a good blaze going and the wind isn't helping,' he added. Those of us in the back of the vehicle all slewed to one side in our seats as he jerkily let out the clutch and pulled quickly away.

Needless to say the journey over the hillside road and down the other side into the valley was hair-raising. At that time of the morning it severely jolted the delicate stomach muscles of those of us who were passengers. Once we were onto the forestry track proper and driving through the woodland it was even more uncomfortable due to the innumerable potholes. As we neared we could see, in the distance, the dancing flames and the smoke belching through the woodland. It was a frightening sight. We all murmured to each other about the daunting task facing us. 'We can walk from here,' McIntosh said. 'I don't want to take the Rover in too close in case a spark sets light to the petrol.'

Warily we all moved forward. With every step we could feel the intensity of the heat getting closer. Even though it was a cold night we hardly needed our working jackets, although superficially they did provide some form of basic fire protection. We were also given safety helmets.

When we'd gone a short way McIntosh stopped and explained the basics of our task. As a group our job was to widen the tree break line. There were existing tree breaks but these were not wide enough, due to the high wind, to prevent the flames from leaping across to the adjacent tree tops on the other side of the break. In conjunction with the lumberjacks we were required to widen the fire breaks to stop the fire from spreading. The lumberjacks were going to fell the trees and cut them into manageable sizes for us to clear away. 'That will give the fire fighters a chance to douse and control the blaze into compartments,' McIntosh explained.

With every step we walked the hotter it became and the more frightening the inferno appeared. We could see close up the wind whipping the flames across the tops of the trees. When we got to the patch where we were going to work it felt as though we had walked into hell. A cacophony of noise surrounded us. Trees and branches were crashing to the ground everywhere. The tree fellers had already started work and the high pitched vibratory sound of their chainsaws added to the confusion of the incessant noise, making normal conversation difficult. McIntosh had to explain our tasks to each of us using mostly sign language. We began to work from the bottom of the tree break upwards.

Soon the surrounding heat and the energy sapping nature of the work became almost impossible to bear. Working in those conditions was exhausting. Quickly I became very tired and strained and needed to sit and rest every ten minutes or so. The approaching flames and the never ending fall of trees around us soon had us up on our feet again.

The tree fellers had started work before us but we had begun to catch them up. That meant we had to stop and wait. Although we were glad of the rest it meant that the flames behind us were creeping up on us. All around us was chaos. It was impossible to speak and be heard. Everything was down to sign language. We had come to a section where we had got quite close to the tree fellers. The whirring sound of their saws added to the other sounds became ear splitting. At least they had ear muffs with their helmets, we didn't. At that moment I was working with my pal Tommy, a local Scottish lad. We were moving quite a bundle of logs further into the wood and out of the fire break. I had my back to the break and could only see into the woodland. When we had downed a log I saw a look of horror cross Tommy's face. He was waving his arms madly at me. I couldn't figure out why. I could see he was also shouting at me but I couldn't hear a word. He began to run towards me. I still couldn't think why.

Unfortunately he was too late. The next thing I knew was a crashing blow on my left shoulder. That was the last thing I remember for some time. I was told later that one of the trees the lumberjack was felling had fallen the wrong way because it had got partly caught up in an adjacent tree on it's way down. They tell me that they had to saw up the fallen tree before they could get me out.

In my absence I'm told my workmates went through hell. They were up there fighting the flames and the damage for over three days before they got the fire under control. In between they were taken home for periodic rests, shower and a change of clothes during which time they were replaced by the workforce from nearby Salen Forestry station. Also they had to bring in fire crews from the mainland in Fort William to help with the flames. In all we lost a hundred acres of mature trees and most of my work mates suffered minor injuries of one form or another. Some were off work for a week or two afterwards.

The next thing I actually remember is waking up in a hospital bed. I was instantly aware of drip feeds, bandages and slings attached to and around and about my arms. At first I found it difficult to focus on anything, everything in front of me appeared to be blurred. At that moment and for some days afterwards I couldn't recall anything that had happened in the forest. The only event that came into my head was McIntosh knocking on the front door of my bungalow and getting me out of bed. Everything that happened after that had gone from my head.

After dozing for some minutes I could eventually see a pretty, brown haired young nurse standing alongside my bed looking down at me. I tried making a smile but I guess it was a pretty weak effort.

'There you are sleepy head,' she said. 'You've been out a long time.'

'Where am I?' I asked and coughed.

'You're in the intensive care unit at the Belford Hospital in Fort William,' she said.

I tried to sit up but the pain was too intense and I gave up the effort. 'What's all this about?' I asked indicating my arms and the drip feeds.

'A tree fell on you during the forest fire. You were knocked out stone cold. You've been here for getting on for two days and this is the first time you've woken properly, although you have turned your head and moaned and groaned a lot.'

'Oh, what are my injuries then?' I continued.

'We don't know all of them, because you've had concussion and we couldn't move you. We do know that you've either broken or dislocated your shoulder and you have lots of other injuries all over your body. When it's safe to move you we can check properly. In the meantime I shouldn't move too much or everything will hurt even more.'

'What about my dog, Bella?' I shouted, it was the first cohesive thought that had come into my head.

'The forestry commission phoned. They said they had taken a locksmith to your bungalow and then taken her to your friends Bob and Jessie.'

Pretty soon after that I must have fallen asleep again because I don't remember much else until what must have been the next morning. Then there was a doctor standing over me at the bedside with the pretty nurse standing alongside him. 'There you are soldier,' he began. 'You've survived then?'

'Have I?' I responded.

'It was a pretty rough do in the forest. You're lucky to be alive. A big tree fell on top of you. Not many would survive that. They're still fighting the fire over there.' At that time I still couldn't remember anything about the whole episode. He went on to say that they would keep me on painkillers for a while and feed me through drips. 'We can't let you eat for a day or so in case we have to operate. In the meantime I suggest you rest as much as possible. If there's anything you want I have no doubt that this young lady will help you.' He looked at her and she blushed, then they were both gone and I fell back into a deep sleep.

That's how it was for the next day or so. They did change my drips and things but in between I slept. Then in the middle of the day orderlies came to fetch me to take x-rays and scans. Attempting to keep still for a long time for the scan was pretty painful and trying. I was glad to get back to my ward and the more comfortable attentions of Janice, who had become my permanent nurse, except for nights, when she was off duty.

The results of the tests showed I had a dislocated left shoulder which would need an operation to reset. A fractured wrist that would have to be put into plaster and various other massive bruises were highlighted which were beginning to hurt painfully, despite the morphine I was on.

Then one day I had a big shock. By then I was, with the aid of mountains of pillows and bolsters, sitting up in bed. I was due to be operated on the following day. It was early afternoon when I spotted, coming down the passageway towards me, a shock of blonde hair. Instantly I knew it was Carol McLeod. I had no time to tidy myself up. Many days growth of beard covered my unshaven face. I don't know what state my hair was in because I couldn't recall putting a comb through it since I had been there.

She beat me to the punch. 'How's the invalid then?' she asked, looking pretty dazzling. Taking her raincoat off revealed a flowery blouse and a red short skirt underneath. I suddenly felt better than I had for a long time.

'Oh, struggling,' I said, 'but I'm much better for seeing you. How did you know I was here?' I offered her to sit in the chair alongside the bed. When she crossed her legs to reveal most of their slender length I felt even better. Suddenly the dull ache in my head wasn't so prominent.

'Oh everybody on the peninsular knows all about you now. They all say it is a miracle that you are still alive. Even the experienced foresters say not many men survive an accident like that. So I came to check for myself to see that you are still with us.'

Carol went on to describe more of the events that had occurred in the forest that fateful night. As she talked she kept tossing back her long blonde tresses. She said details of the blaze had been featured on the main Scottish news, but the inferno was still smoking and a fire crew remained up there as occasionally flames did keep flaring up in the wind. Two or three of the other lads had received injuries and were off work but didn't require hospital treatment. Doctor Masson and the district nurse were being kept busy.

We continued to talk about matters in general for a further ten minutes or so then I spotted Janice coming down the passageway towards us. 'Oh look out the boss is coming,' I said to Carol.

The nurse entered the ward with a scowl on her face. 'Come on now Gareth we can't have you getting tired, this is your first visitor.' I looked at Carol, she looked back at me and smiled, then got up to kiss me on the cheek. I saw a look of jealousy cross Janice's face.

'I'll call in and see you when you've had your operation,' Carol said and I watched her click clack away on her high heels, across the ward.

Janice then began to fuss round me like an old hen. 'You're only just out of a serious accident and still in intensive care,' she said. 'You must rest.'

I smiled and closed my eyes.

* * * * *

I have to say that the operation was hell. Not the actual hour or so that I spent under the anaesthetic, because throughout that I was knocked completely out and knew nothing about it. It was the recovery and the aftermath that brought the real trauma. Once the anaesthetic and the initial morphine injection had worn off the sheer agony of everything set in throughout my body. I was only allowed to take painkillers every four hours and once they had passed the three hour mark I had to suffer increasing pain. Repeatedly I asked Janice and the other nurses to give me another dose, but my pleas were met with 'You've got twenty minutes to go before you can have any more,' and similar phrases of defiance. The night time proved to be more hellish than the day as there were less interruptions from the nurses and the other orderlies as a distraction.

Two days after the op, when I was feeling pretty groggy and low, I received another visitor. This time it was McIntosh from the commission.

'How are you son?' he asked when he walked towards me. I was glad I was unable to shake hands with him as he possessed an iron like grip.

'Pretty fed up,' I replied.

'Well you've done very well to get this far. Not many men would have survived the accident you had. They tell me you've just about been behaving yourself so far in here. You haven't been flirting with any of the nurses yet, have you?'

'I don't think I would be capable of that at the moment.'

'Just as well,' McIntosh responded chuckling. 'Anyway I told them you're a Welshman not a local Scotsman and that if they have any trouble to kick you out immediately.' We both laughed, which was the first time I had done that properly since I had been there.

He went on to tell me about the other lads who had been injured and described their injuries. He said the fire was just about out but somebody was up there all day and night just to keep a check on it. In a short while he was gone and afterwards I was again exhausted.

A couple of days later I received another more glamorous visitor. Carol McLeod returned looking succulently sexy. Removing her sheepskin short jacket revealed a white tight fitting sweater and a short red miniskirt. Fortunately by then I was feeling a little better, had managed a shave and combed my hair and was more or less sitting upright.

'Well you look a little better,' she began. I confirmed that I felt that way.

'Have they given you a date to come out yet?' she said next. Her blue eyes were quite penetrating.

'Not for another week at least, I think,' I replied. 'They are worried about me being at home alone when I am so weak. I've asked Janice the nurse if she will come and stay with me but she says she's not allowed to do that.'

'Well I can call in and see you every day and I'll get your shopping.'

My mind went into overdrive and began to spin in a whirl. 'Well that's very kind of you,' I responded. 'I think the district nurse is going to call on me every day and check on my bandages and dressings and there is talk of organising a carer to come in each day to help.'

'Good. I'll still come and see you anyway.'

'I'd be grateful.' I replied.

We talked some more about events in the village and the repercussions of the fire. Then, after kissing me on the cheek she was gone, although her perfume lingered around my bed for some time afterwards.

When Janice next came to attend to me I said to her. 'Instead of all these carers coming to see me when I'm home couldn't you come and stay with me for a week or so? You know what's wrong with me.'

'P'h,' she responded. 'From what I've seen you've got enough help over there already,' then stomped off out of the ward.

Then a couple of days later I had another surprise visitor. I looked up from reading my newspaper to see Jack Banyard striding into the ward wearing his police uniform. 'How are you boy?' he asked. I related the details as he sat down by the bed.

'That was a rum do,' he responded. 'You were lucky to get out of that one alive, many haven't. I had some police business in the Fort so thought I had better check up on you.'

We talked some more for another ten minutes before he made moves to leave. As he was about to depart he turned around and said, 'I'll call in and see you when you're home, but if there's anything you need once you get there don't hesitate to contact me.' Then he was gone.

I suppose that was my first real example of how the locals would rally round to help anybody who was in real trouble whatever their nationality or creed.

CHAPTER TWELVE

In all I was in the Belford for the best part of a fortnight. Most of the time, except for Janice's attentions, it was a painful and tiring business. Each night, for all the time I was there, I received an injection into my buttocks which was extremely painful, and made my rear end sore, increased my bad temper and made it difficult to get off to sleep. Gradually I came off the drip feeds and my arm was put in a sling, as well as a plaster on my wrist. They also began to walk me around the wards with the aid of a stick, which I would need to use when I got home. Over those days I also had a couple of visits from some of the other lads in the forestry squad. They were the ones who were still off work because of their injuries. We morbidly compared notes about our various ailments.

As the day of my discharge grew nearer Janice began to fuss over me even more. She provided me with enough medical items and tablets to last me for what seemed like six months. She also wrote out endless lists for me as to how many tablets I had to take and when. How I was going to cope with all of that on my own I couldn't figure out. When the day arrived we exchanged a cheek kiss and she saw me down to the ambulance. By then, with the aid of the stick, I was walking quite well. Before I climbed into the ambulance I gave her a big hug and thanked her for everything she had done for me. 'You take care of yourself now,' were her final remarks to me. Looking back on it I suppose Janice was the best woman I had known since Anne.

Thankfully the district nurse was awaiting me at my bungalow when I reached home. The Forestry had given her a copy of the new key which she passed on to me. Instantly I felt how cold the property was, having been unoccupied for so long. We firstly went round each room switching on all the fires. I noticed that somebody had brought in some wood for the wood fire. She had brought me a meal from the nursing home canteen and helped unpack my belongings before settling me down to eat. She said that a carer would be there to see to me later on. Then she was gone saying she would be back during the following day. The problems of existing out of hospital without Janice's help soon became pretty evident. Trying to eat a cooked meal with only one workable hand was extremely difficult and laborious. I was told to leave the washing up as the carer would see to that and the nurse would collect the dishes on her next visit. After eating, all I could really manage to do was to turn up the fire and crash out on the lounge settee. I was awoken by a hammering on the front door. I looked at my watch and discovered that it was five o'clock.

Standing upright was difficult and I almost fell back down on the settee, which jarred my shoulder. Taking a little more time I was eventually able to slowly and dizzily stumble to the front door. Outside, in the rain stood Mary, my carer. A more redoubtably strong, grey haired woman in her mid fifties, I had yet to meet. My first thoughts were that if she had to lift me into bed that she would be perfectly capable of doing so. As soon as she walked through the door she took over the place. Instantly she began to tidy up my clutter. She wanted to know, 'where my clothes for the night were. What clean clothes did I want for the next day.' She demanded the clothes I was standing up in which she would take home and launder. She turned down the bed cleared the washing up and ran the Hoover around most of the rooms.

'So I don't have to get you out of bed in the morning, you'd better give me a key,' she demanded. Fortunately I had a few copies and I gave her one. 'If you want my advice I should get yourself off to bed soon or you may crash out here in the lounge.'

Within a while, having made me a cup of tea, she left saying she would be back at eight in the morning. She was quite right about the procedures to adopt for as soon as I had downed the tea there was little else I could do but crawl into bed. Washing, cleaning my teeth and the normal bed time routines completely exhausted me.

Mary had ensured that I had taken the prescribed tablets. When I put my head on the pillow I instantly thought of Bella. I knew I was in no fit state to cope with her at that stage, but I did miss her presence around the bungalow. Mind you very few thoughts stayed in my head for long after that and I was pretty soon doggo.

* * * * *

My recovery and recuperation was a long, slow and at times painful process. Being on my own a lot of the time with only one useable arm, didn't help the proceedings. My bad temper and irascibility continued throughout most of that period. After the first week or so I was able to get out for some walks, although the inclement weather didn't help in that respect. Regularly I visited Bella at Bob and Jessie's but I had to be careful with her boisterous attention because of my injuries. No way, for some considerable time, could I consider taking her for a proper walk by myself, although quite often she would follow me on my way home and regularly Bob had to come and fetch her. I think she was thoroughly confused by the whole situation. My carer and the district nurse continued to be daily visitors.

Throughout that time the most exciting days were when Carol McLeod came to visit, which happened two or three times a week. During that period she acquired for me most of my food shopping and each time she would stay for about half an hour enlightening me with her glamour, wit and sparkling conversation. There was no doubt that I developed an enormous crush on her, although what she could see in me, particularly in that predicament I couldn't imagine. However I wasn't prepared to do anything that might alter her apparent affection for me. After a few weeks the Forestry took me to Fort William for some physiotherapy treatment, with a view to getting me back into work. Once all my bandages were removed I was able to progress quicker and eventually, much to my relief acquired Bella back.

When it actually came to restarting work it was a different trial altogether. Although for the first week McIntosh put me on light duties, the early morning start and the long days of physical toil resulted in almost total exhaustion. By then Mary, my carer, and the district nurse had ceased to call and I also had Bella to look after and exercise. After the first two days I felt totally washed out and was almost prepared to quit the job. Somehow or other though I managed to keep going, although I couldn't say any of it was enjoyable except for a bit of craic with the lads. If I'm honest the only thing that kept me going was Carol McLeod's two or three visits a week, bringing me my shopping after work. Her calls coincided with picking up her children from school, so she never stayed long as by then they needed feeding and her husband was awaiting her company and his meal at home.

The more we chatted however and the more relaxed she became in my company I began to discover a certain unease she had about her husband. From what she told me their courtship was a very short and I guess a passionate affair. At the time she was very young and working for a fashion magazine in London. It appears she quickly became overwhelmed by Angus' wealth, his masculinity, his glamorous celebrity lifestyle and the famous and important friends, most of whom were in the money making business. The more she talked to me however the more doubts she expressed about how he had actually accumulated all this wealth. Conversely she said he was wonderful with her when in Scotland with her and the children, but it was what he got up to when he was away from there that worried her. As a result I remained in a confused state of mind about our relationship.

To add to my dilemma, one morning, early, when I was taking Bella around the garden for her early morning call, I noticed that a posy of flowers had been tied to the handle of the back door of the bungalow. On inspecting them I realised they were not the type of flowers you would buy from a shop or grow in a normal garden. They were definitely wild mountain flowers, picked on a hillside somewhere. That meant only one thing. They must have been brought there by Mhairi, for she was the only person who used the back door to my bungalow, after climbing over the back fence so as not to be seen. I guessed she must have somehow or another found out about my injuries, although Bob and Jessie still hadn't seen anything of her for a long time.

Very slowly the days and the weeks ticked by. The effort of work, Bella and normal living requirements were more than enough to cope with and most days I usually crashed out in bed long before my normal bed time hours. Many times I considered going up into the mountains at the weekend to try and see Mhairi, but I'm afraid the thought of that steep mountain path put me off the idea and I had enough female company to cope with as a result of Carol's regular visits. The more often she called the closer we became, both mentally and I have to say physically. There were many occasions when I had to restrain myself from wanting to reach out and touch her very nubile body. Goodbye kisses, although they remained on a cheek to cheek basis, our bodies gradually became closer and more entangled.

Also, as time went by, she opened up to me more and more of her concerns about Angus. She told me that occasionally when he wasn't there, although she wasn't supposed to, she did open some of his mail. Much of it was about the estate, but there was the odd letter or two about the diminishing value of his investments and she said that it did worry her. At that particular time the financial markets were going through one of their periodic big dips. Although it didn't effect me personally, from what I read in the newspaper and saw on the television, millions of pounds were being wiped off the value of shares and all other forms of investments. I did therefore try to console Carol by saying that all these things were cyclical and it wouldn't be long before the markets were riding high again, but I could see she was worried.

One day I was working on the hillside. By then I was back to full duties with the fencing gang and we were up at a spot a little over twelve hundred feet up on the mountain side. The skies were, for once, clear. Suddenly some distance below us I spotted a figure move in the wood. As before it was difficult to detect who it was as the person kept darting in and out behind the trees, but there was no doubt that, whoever it was, was watching me. In my mind I knew it was Mhairi, although I couldn't be absolutely sure. If it was her she somehow looked different in shape and size. After a few moments the figure was gone and I didn't see it again that day. When I got home that evening I couldn't stop thinking about it and the image stayed in my mind throughout my sleeping hours. By the morning I had made the decision to try and get up to her cave at the weekend.

On the way there, if I didn't enjoy the walk and climb, because of the remnants of my injuries, at least Bella did. It was the first time since I had been in hospital that she was properly out loose without the lead in open moorland and she enjoyed herself to the full, crashing through streams, bracken and the undergrowth. My progress was more slow and ponderous. It was obvious to me that I still hadn't recovered completely from the aftermath of my hospitalisation.

By the time I got near to the cave I could see smoke emitting from it's aperture. Then when I got closer I could see Mhairi standing at the entrance. She must have spotted me on the way up. She didn't actually wave to me, but there did appear to be a look of welcome on her face. As soon as Bella caught sight and scent of her she left me and went charging up on her own to where Mhairi stood. Once they were reunited the dog jumped up at her and they made a big fuss of each other. It took me another good five minutes or more to get to where they both were standing. Now I could see her properly it was obvious that Mhairi was the person I'd spotted in the wood the other day, as she was wearing the same clothes.

She had changed in appearance though. She looked much stouter, her normally gaunt thin face had become rounded, although the moon and stars was still emblazoned on her forehead. She was wearing a very loose fitting dress, I could see that there was a bulge protruding from her stomach. This time she couldn't hide the fact that she was pregnant.

'How are you?' I asked. 'You look well.'

In response she muttered many phrases of her gobbledegook language, with lots of 'Machrehanish's, Mackrenscables, and much more. At least she said it with a smile on her face. She and Bella continued their party of mutual affection, mostly ignoring me.

Eventually I was offered a seat on the cushions and some herbal tea. After I'd sat down and taken the first sip I said, 'Well you can't deny to me now that you are pregnant?' Bella had stretched out alongside her with her head on her paws.

'What if I am? What's it got to do with you?'

'I would say quite a lot if I am the father.'

'How do you know that? You are assuming an awful lot.'

'Maybe I am but whatever you can't have the baby up here. It's not safe.'

'The deer and all the other animals have their babies up here. They seem to manage OK. Why shouldn't I?'

'Mhairi you're not a wild animal, you're a human being and your body has different needs.'

'Pah,' she responded.

'Well whether it's my child or not, why don't you come and stay at my place when the time is near. At least there you will have some warmth and comfort, even if it's only for the child's sake.'

She repeated the 'Pah,' then went on to ask me about my accident and my injuries.

'How did you know about that?' I asked.

'Oh, eventually I get to know everything in these parts. Actually I overheard the Forestry men talking about it when I was down in the wood once. They said you were quite ill.'

'Was it you who put the flowers on my back door?'

She wasn't answering that either and continued to sup her tea, but the more she relaxed in my company the more we began to talk more openly. She was inquisitive to know about my hospitalisation and what they actually did to me there. In time she said, 'I told you the trees would punish you for chopping them down. They don't like it, I promise you.' Regrettably I could find no suitable answer to that.

Eventually it was time for me to go. We exchanged kisses on the cheeks. I said, 'Why don't you come down and see me sometime. And Bob and Jessie haven't seen you for weeks. They are missing you.'

'We'll see,' was her reply.

She and Bella made another big fuss of each other before the dog and I made our way back down the mountain.

Thoughts of our conversation and Mhairi's physical condition played on my mind for the next few days. If I'm truthful I really didn't know how to handle the situation. I was convinced, maybe wrongly, that the child was mine, but there was no way of proving it and she certainly wasn't going to tell me.

During that week I learnt of more troubles locally that were to occupy my thoughts. During one of her periodic late afternoon visits Carol McLeod confided to me that she was getting more and more worried about the financial mess that her husband Angus seemed to be getting into. She said I was the only one she could talk to about it as she knew I had been a journalist and would have some knowledge about these matters. She told me that one day when Angus was out she received a telephone call from a bank asking her to get Angus to contact them immediately as his account was getting into trouble. 'We do have a joint account,' she continued, 'and I know that is all right because I use it every day for the housekeeping and I continually check the balance. But this must be some other bank as they wouldn't speak to me about the problem as they said I wasn't a party to the account. Gareth I am worried. I know he dabbles a lot in finance when he is in London and I know nothing about those dealings. When I have asked recently he tells me not to worry my pretty little head about such things. He says that as long as me and the children are all right that's all that matters, but I am worried and I do care. What do you think I should do?'

Although I wanted to help her it was really none of my business. What goes on between a husband and wife, financially or otherwise should remain between the two of them. From my days in journalism I had witnessed and reported on lots of bust ups between husbands and wives, particularly when there were large sums of money involved. I had to be careful in what I said because although I valued Carol's friendship and help greatly, there was no way I could, or should, become involved between her and Angus, that would be just asking for big trouble.

However, she seemed to want to persist in laying her soul open to me on these matters. Each time she visited I received a mini tirade about her woes on the subject matter. Then one time she arrived with details of one of the banks that were hounding them. I have to admit that I had never heard of them and they certainly weren't one of the well known British clearing banks.

When I confessed that I knew nothing about them she retorted that, 'Perhaps some of your ex-friends and colleagues in the newspaper business might know.' I was reluctant to say that I didn't have many ex-friends in that connection and also that most of my ex-colleagues wouldn't want to talk to me again.

When she was gone I was in a quandary about what to do. Since I had been in the village Carol had been so good to me. Firstly she had arranged for me to undertake the fencing projects around their estate, which was a definite help with my finances. Then since my hospitalisation she had visited me regularly and got in for me most of my basic shopping requirements. So no way did I want to turn her down flat when she came to me for help. Also clouding it all was this feeling of physical attraction between us which I am sure was not just on my part. I thought that there was no other reason why a woman in her position would want to spend so much time around a bloke who until recent times had been a perfect stranger and, in economic terms, almost a down and out.

I therefore gave the matter a lot of thought. Living up there in the western highlands I had completely lost touch with the current machinations in the financial world. Where I lived, except for the McLeod's, everybody was on low incomes and survived on basic standards. What they got up to in London, Frankfurt and New York could have been on another planet as far as we were concerned.

CHAPTER THIRTEEN

Over the following days I racked my brains as to who I could contact in that respect. As I have said before, nearly all of my ex-working colleagues would have nothing to do with me as most of them still thought that I had molested Janet Lawrence in some way or another. One by one, in my mind, I went through them and ticked each one off as being no help to me on this matter.

It was really only when I had nearly given up racking my brains I belatedly settled on someone I had completely forgotten about. His name was Charles Watson. He actually had worked in the financial reporting side of the newspaper but when there was an office booze up, to celebrate one event or another, he and I would often end up sitting together and in an alcoholic sort of way we would try and put the world to rights. The other advantage was that Charles had retired some time before the events with Janet blew up. I did, however, remember that in retirement he still worked as a freelance financial journalist so I guessed that he would still be in touch with what was going on in that world. In fact his articles still sometimes appeared in the newspaper.

How to contact him was the problem. Firstly I had no phone. The one public phone half way up the mountain was totally inadequate for my purposes of talking to a financial expert in Cardiff. Those practicalities occupied my mind for many hours. And where did Charles Watson live? I had no idea of his current whereabouts let alone his telephone number. When Carol next called I presented my dilemma to her. 'I want to try and help,' I said, then illustrated my problem.

'There's no problem with that,' she responded. 'When Angus is out for the day, you can use our phone at home.'

So after a couple of days and further brain searching I arranged with Carol a time when it would be convenient for me to visit their house. I still had trepidations about the matter and continued to feel guilty and unsure about coming between a man and his wife and getting involved in their affairs. She had arranged a time for mid-Saturday morning and told me that Angus would be gone to Glasgow for the day with the children and would not be back until that evening.

I was greeted by her in the kitchen of the big house and then guided through to a spacious lounge furnished with large expensive armchairs and sofas. Occasional tables and glass cabinets filled up the rest of the space and there was a large picture window at the front with views across the valley. The room was carpeted with a pile deep enough to lose yourself in. Carol's blonde hair was arranged long and flowing. A tight fitting sweater exemplified the top half of her body and a short miniskirt did the same for her legs. Instantly my mind was on more erotic things than contacting Charles Watson.

'It is good of you to help me with this,' she said as she pointed me towards one of the large sofas.

'But I still don't want to come between you and Angus,' I responded as I sat down.

'I know, but as his wife and the mother of his children I have a duty to find out what is going on, as, if there is trouble, it's going to affect all of us. And I may be able to help. I'm not completely stupid, although I sometimes wonder if Angus thinks I am.'

She sat down beside me. In doing so her miniskirt slid up her legs to her thighs. I felt something more than horny and was having trouble controlling it. On the occasional table beside the sofa was a telephone and she reached across me to pick up the receiver. In the process her blonde hair brushed across my face and her hand rested on my thigh to steady herself as she lifted the heavy phone from the small table. Further convulsions swept through my body, like the fire that had swept through the forest on that fateful night.

Fortunately I still had the main telephone number of my previous employers amongst my papers at home. I dialled it with trepidation. Miraculously a voice I recognised answered.

'Alison?' I ventured. 'Is that you? It's Gareth Rees. Do you remember me?'

'Of course I do,' she replied. Thankfully she was one of the few people who still liked me when I left there. Probably because she hated Janet Lawrence. I think they had fallen out a long time back, I guess over another man. 'How are you?' she continued. 'I haven't heard from you for yonks.' For a few minutes we exchanged information about our recent history. I was however, concerned about burning up Carol's phone bill and I soon intervened.

'Alison,' I said. 'I know I'm not supposed to ask you these things, but I know that Charles Watson is still writing articles for the paper and so is still in touch with the financial world. At the moment I have a big financial problem and he is the only man I can think of to talk to about it, but I have no idea where he is living at the moment. You couldn't possibly let me know his telephone number,' I continued. 'I know I'm asking a big favour.' For a moment there was silence on the line.

'Let me see what I can find,' Alison said.

She was gone off the line for a while. In the interim I winked at Carol. She responded by giving me a full kiss on my cheek. Again I began struggling with controlling my erection.

'I think I've found something,' Alison said, when she came back on the line. 'He now lives in Penarth.' She gave me his home phone number.

'I owe you Alison,' I said.

'Good,' she replied.

I repeated my gratitude and followed with. 'I'll buy you a lunch when I'm next in Cardiff.'

'I'll hold you to that,' Alison said and we rang off.

By the time I finished the call I realised that Carol had her right arm hooked around my left one and her right thigh was pressing into my body. Whilst my luck is in I thought I would give Charles Watson's number a call. As it was a Saturday morning I guessed it might be a good time to catch him at home. To dial the number I had to unhook my arm from Carol's, but she placed her elbow on my shoulder and her hand rested on my neck. I needed to concentrate harder to dial the correct number.

It rang for a long time. I was about to hang up when a powerful voice I recognised answered with the words, 'Charles Watson.'

'Charles,' I responded. 'It's Gareth Rees. I used to work with you on the paper, do you remember? We used to share a few jars together when the time was right.'

'Of course I do dear boy,' he said. 'I heard you'd skedaddled off to Scotland or somewhere remote like that.'

I confirmed he was correct, but quickly got to the nub of the matter. I said that a lady friend was concerned about the investments her husband had made. I told him that they had two young children and she was worried that he had got their money into trouble. Banks had been phoning their home regularly asking to speak to him.

'Well Gareth,' Charles replied. 'You know the financial markets have dived, almost collapsed recently. Everybody's investments are down badly, even mine.'

'I've read about that,' I responded, 'but she tells me her normal bank account is OK because she is still using that and knows it's in credit. What else could it be?' By then I could feel Carol's hand stroking the back of my neck.

'People invest in all sorts of crazy things nowadays. Some folks trade in things called futures or hedge funds, which means that they really take a bet with their money on whether the markets go up or down. It's a bit like betting on the horses, if they get it right they can make a fortune. If they get it wrong they can lose everything. Unfortunately financial advisers have been pushing these things recently to wealthy punters, but at this moment their net worths are practically useless for the amount they have invested. Some people have lost millions.'

'How can my friend find out how much he's in for and who the money is invested with?' I asked. 'I mean she's not a party to any of it.'

'The only way she can do that is to get her husband to confess or find some paper work relating to the investment.'

'I don't think he'll tell her anything until they are destitute,' I said.

For a moment there was silence on the line, then Charles said, 'I'll tell you what I'll do Gareth. I'll send you a copy of the Financial Times in which all these funds are listed. But there are hundreds of them. She won't get any positive information until we know which fund he is involved with.'

I gave him my address and he agreed to post the details on. 'I'm grateful Charles,' I said. 'When I have found out some more information can I come back to you?'

'Of course you can dear boy,' Charles replied, 'but I'll expect a bottle of McAllan's best malt next time I see you.'

'I'll do my best Charles,' I said and we made our farewells and rang off.

I related to Carol the gist of our conversation. She was still stroking the back of my neck as I talked. 'I'll see what I can find around the house,' she said.

The stroking of my neck was beginning to get to me, so to save any more real trouble I made some excuse about having to take Bella out for her morning walk. As I left, in the hallway, Carol moved towards me, then into my arms and kissed me fully on the lips. It was a passionate kiss. Fireworks were going off in my head.

'I am grateful to you Gareth,' she said and added 'I'll be in touch with you next week.' I left her house in haste.

CHAPTER FOURTEEN

Later in the following week a letter arrived from Charles Watson with a couple of pages from the Financial Times showing the investment schemes he felt Angus could have invested in. As he had intimated there were literally hundreds of them. In his letter he confirmed that without knowing the particular plan involved it would be impossible to speculate further. As he had also said a minus sign was attached to the growth of nearly all the schemes illustrated in those pages. The possibilities bedevilled my mind for a few days while I was in work. We were by then working on the downward slope of the fence line, and in some ways this was more difficult and tiring than working on the upward one. My knees creaked and ached all day and afterwards as we tackled the downward slope.

One day, later in the week after I had returned from work, Carol called in at my bungalow with some groceries she knew I needed. After our last farewell at her house I was careful, but sat near her on the sofa. It didn't however stop her from regularly tossing her long blonde hair around her head and revealing another big show of her legs and thighs when she sat down.

'You're going to think me very wicked,' she said after we had exchanged pleasantries on the state of our respective health. Of that I had no doubts. 'But I have managed to open my husband's desk drawer,' she continued. 'Thankfully, for my sake the desk is very old. I think it was his father's before him. Anyway, with the slimmest kitchen knife I possess, I have managed to get under the lock and prise the drawer open.' My mind boggled at the thought of what this woman might do next. 'And do you know what I have found?' she said, holding up three pieces of printed paper. She handed them over to me and in doing so I received another erotic shot of the aroma from her perfume.

The foolscap sheets she had passed to me were stapled together and headed by the company's name, Ocean Investments, and their logo. On inspecting them I could see they were addressed to Angus alone and were obviously a quarterly report of investments held in the headed company's name. The list showed investment funds in various different markets, many of them overseas. At the bottom of the last sheet I could see that in total the sum of money amounted to over seventy thousand pounds. On seeing this I looked up at Carol. 'Yes I know it's a lot isn't it?' she said when she caught my glance. In response I just shook my head in amazement.

When I inspected the papers more carefully I could see that against the total of every particular fund there was a minus sign, followed by a figure which exceeded at least a twenty five per cent downfall in nearly every case. Looking more carefully I noticed that at the beginning of the statement was a figure that was in excess of one hundred and thirty thousand pounds which was obviously the figure carried forward from the previous statement. Therefore, as Carol had guessed there had been a dramatic fall in Angus' investments.

When I illustrated all this to her she responded with, 'I told you something like this was going on, but what am I going to do about it. This statement is two months old. The money could have gone down even further since then,' she added.

I thought for a moment before replying. 'I don't see that there is a lot you can do about it except confront Angus with it.' For once her face remained impassive and silent. 'Carol I really think you have two choices,' I continued. 'You can either ignore it and hope he sorts it out or you can tell him you know and face the consequences.'

'H'm,' she responded. 'If I tell him I know about it, it could end my marriage. He a bit funny like that. He doesn't like me dabbling in his private matters. If he kicks me out I have nothing else to fall back on. Without him I am worthless, income wise.'

I thought for some moments. Her sharp blue eyes were fixed on mine, which unnerved me slightly. 'Well you could say you discovered it from these telephone calls you keep getting,' I said eventually. 'You could say one of them let slip that his funds had gone down dramatically, but let me speak to Charles Watson about it first. He knows more about these things than I do.'

We both agreed to that. As before, when she made to leave I received another passionate kiss on my lips. If I'm honest I have to confess I was enjoying them.

For the rest of the following day I was perplexed about what to do on this matter. I had a big surprise though later on when I passed Bob and Jessie's house on my evening walk with Bella. Bob was waiting for me at his front gate on my way back to my bungalow. Bella made a big fuss of him jumping up on her back legs to get at him over the top of his gate. 'There you are,' he said in his soft lilting highland accent. 'I thought I ought to tell you that I saw Mhairi today. I was up in yonder woodland collecting some timber windblows when I saw her,' he said pointing in the direction of the wood. 'I think she must have spotted me first, but she came over to see me anyway.'

'How did she look?' I asked.

'She looked OK,' he paused. 'I don't know a lot about these things but I would swear to God that she was pregnant. She was wearing lots of loose clothes wrapped around her body, you know the sort of things she wears, so I couldn't see her outline properly, but her face was definitely rounder and chubbier.'

'What did she say about not coming to see you?'

'Oh not much. You know what she is like. Something about being busy. Goodness know what she gets up to up there by herself, but that's how she is. I just thought I should let you know, as you've been asking.'

'She's a strange one, that girl, all right,' I replied. 'But thanks for telling me.' We talked some more about the weather, then I continued on my way home with Bella, with my head full of more thoughts.

What to do about Carol's revelations troubled me. I discovered Ocean Investments listed on the pages Charles Watson had sent me. From what I saw if I had had my money invested with them I would have been really worried. All their funds looked in a pretty dire state. Really I needed to talk to Charles about it. The only way for me to get hold of him and discuss the matter properly was by telephone, which I didn't have. The phone on the road over the mountain was completely impractical for such a lengthy conversation. If I went to Carol's house again I would run the gauntlet of being sexually propositioned by her.

Eventually I remembered that the hotel in the village, which was my Friday night bolt hole, had a telephone cubicle which meant that I could at least speak to Charles in private and there was also a light in the booth, unlike the phone box on the side of the mountain road. I didn't go down to the hotel every Friday night, as the locals all drank too much for me, which usually caused me to have a hangover on the Saturday morning when I might have some fencing work to do at the McLeod's. I decided to go down to the hotel on the Saturday morning and save myself some money as the phone call was going to be quite costly. I knew the hotel would be about to open and I could badger Roger, the landlord, for some loose change to use on the phone. And it was a time I had caught Charles in on my last call to him.

Eventually after pouring a stream of money into the phone, I heard Charles respond on the other end of the line. I was so unused to phones that I had initially forgotten to press button B on the telephone box, which you had to do in those days to connect. Thankfully I managed to do that before Charles rang off.

We exchange pleasantries then I told him about Ocean Investments. He didn't know any details of the fund but said he would make enquiries. How to get back to me with any details was the problem. The postal service to the highlands would take too long. I suggested that he ring the hotel and get Roger to tell me, then I would phone him back as soon as was convenient to both of us. That required me to buy Roger a drink to convey the message to me. Nothing was easy in the highlands and everything took a long time. Patience was essential if you wished to survive there with your mindset in tact.

One day, after work, Roger's wife Sandra called in at my bungalow after picking her kids up from school. 'There's been a message from your friend Charles Watson,' she said, she was short, plump, middle aged with closely cropped ginger hair. 'He says he will be at home this evening if you want to phone him,' I thanked her and said I would be down to the hotel later that evening.

As I walked down the single track road that night I could see the lights on at the McLeods' place and wondered what would be going on over there. I had made sure to take plenty of money with me to the hotel as no doubt I would have to buy somebody I knew a drink as I went through the bar. Fortunately it was early and so I was able to sneak through to the phone booth without anybody spotting me. Charles answered and this time I remembered to press button B.

'I've managed to make some enquiries on Ocean Investments,' he said after our initial pleasantries. 'From what I can find out their funds are fairly volatile. In the good days they did increase by thirty or forty percent, but it seems that in the current difficult market they have fallen by even more than that, so your neighbour may well have less in there than he put in to start with. I warned you that this is the trouble with these types of funds. They are highly speculative, even in the good times. Also speaking to people I know, they tell me that their salesmen are very aggressive. My pals say that you should really only put a small portion of your savings into something like this as it's a gamble. You should then spread the rest into other safer investments. The trouble is that their sales people somehow manage to find out how much savings you have in total and it seems they persuade their clients to invest the lot with them. I'm afraid people are becoming gullible because of the greed factor. The salesman will show them growth figures from the good times and the clients get taken in by it all.'

We talked some more on the subject, then I asked, 'What do you think he should do Charles? Should he cash it all in now?'

'Well if he does he might not get what he put in back. It might be better to wait until the markets improve, but that could take a long time. He might have to wait a few years for that to happen.'

We continued to talk until my money ran out, then I thanked him and he told me to keep in touch. 'I'll be awaiting on that bottle of highland malt,' he said before he rang off.

I still wasn't sure about what to say to Carol on the matter when I next saw her, but I didn't have to wait long for that opportunity. She called round to see me with some shopping after school on the Monday, flouncing into my lounge whilst swishing her long blonde hair near my face.

'Have you heard anything from your investment pal?' she asked, whilst fixing her best blue eyed stare on me.

'I have, over the weekend,' I replied, 'but it's not very good news. I'm afraid all of Ocean Investments have crashed badly. His fund is now probably far less than what he put in,' I continued.

Her blue eyes were by then staring at me starkly. 'What should we do, or better still what should he do? What did your pal say about that?' I repeated what Charles had said to me. 'Oh dear I thought he was in a mess,' she replied. 'Around the house he's gone very quiet. He's not been his normal ebullient self at all.'

'Well, as I said before you really have two choices. You can either confront him with what you know or say nothing and let him get on with it. What did you do with the copy of the report you found?'

'Oh I put it back in his desk drawer and sealed the lock back up again. I was sure he would spot it was missing if I didn't do that. I'm not just a pretty face you know.'

'I'm beginning to realise that,' I responded. 'You must do what you think best Carol I can't really advise you on that one. You know the man better than I do.'

We left it at that. She left giving me another passionate kiss on the lips.

'I'm sorry to have troubled you with all this,' she said as she went out through the door.

'It's no problem,' I replied. 'That's what friends are for.' Before she disappeared she turned her head around and gave me another glowing look. When she was gone her perfume still lingered in the room for some time.

CHAPTER FIFTEEN

That weekend there was an annual event in the village which had become quite a social occasion. Once a year, as the winter weather set in, the lady who owned the village post office, Mrs McFadyen, used to organise for coal to be delivered to her shop. What made it such an occasion was that the cargo was delivered by what came to be referred to as the 'puffer,' an old dilapidated steam, cargo boat from Fort William. On a Saturday, in early winter, it used to cross Loch Linnhe and dock on the harbour key outside her premises to unload it's black shiny cargo of coal. The event began in the days when the ferry to the Fort was only small and not big enough to take a large coal lorry. Mrs McFadyen would then sell the coal on to the locals by the sack full. In those bygone days this was the only reliable source of fuel the villagers could obtain to heat their homes in the cold weather. Before that they had to rely on peat which they needed to dig from the land and dry out in the summer months, or collect timber that had been blown down in the gales. Usually on the day when the 'puffer' arrived the forestry work force would help out with the bagging of the coal on the quayside and barrow it into Mrs McFadyen's outside covered area. She did pay ten pounds to each helper in the task and so being short of money I was only too pleased to help out.

In those days the event had become quite a tourist attraction and that Saturday scores of them were scattered around the shop with cameras at the ready. With all the other forestry lads I turned up at about half past seven to watch the boat come in. Thankfully that Saturday morning turned out to be bright, clear and sunny. The loch was calm and the old steamer looked a picturesque sight as she approached the harbour, an almost surreal vision from the past. The skipper sounded the ship's hooter several times as he closed in on the quay. Somehow it all didn't fit in with the modern world my age group had grown up into. As well as us lads a few enthusiastic amateur photographers had also turned out at that early hour to capture the image. They clicked away merrily as the boat closed in on the quay. The coal was unloaded by the boat's skipper using a small ancient, rusty crane which was housed on it's upper deck.

As the pile of coal grew bigger we lads set about bagging it and then taking the bags by the barrow load to the shelter of Mrs McFadyen's outside store. It was hard, back breaking work and we were all soon down to our shirtsleeves and sweating profusely. Throughout the morning more and more locals and tourists began to gather around the harbour, armed with cameras and cine cameras. In amongst them I spotted the flash of Carol's blonde hair. She was with the children, but most of the time she appeared to be pointing her cine at me. By eleven thirty we lads were exhausted. However, true to the spirit of the village, Roger from the hotel appeared, with jugs filled with beer, and glasses. It was badly needed and most appreciated and it did give us the impetus to carry on and finish the task.

It was after midday by the time we'd swept up and hosed down the harbour quay. After that all us workers were only fit enough to struggle up to the hotel bar and imbibe in more pint glasses of the same refreshing alcoholic liquid. As a result I spent most of the ten pounds Mrs McFadyen had given us. It was a tiring walk back to my bungalow, where, after letting Bella out around the garden, I crashed out on my bed and slept for the rest of the afternoon.

* * * * *

During the following week my mind told me that somehow I had allowed two women into my life at the same time, something I had never done before. As I have already stated, from the time I met Anne there was really no other woman in my life and my experience with Janet Lawrence had put me off any further relationships. But at that moment I had to confess that I both liked and was attracted to Carol and Mhairi. It was a conundrum that I really didn't know how to handle. For her part Mhairi did keep well away from me, although that didn't stop me thinking about her every day. Whereas Carol seemed determined to encroach on my life no matter what it took. I was therefore not surprised to see her Range Rover pull up outside my bungalow early in the following week.

I watched her make her way to my front door, dressed to kill, and I tried to get my mind into some kind of order to deal with whatever matter she may bring up.

'You're looking very glamorous,' I ventured as she approached.

'Well I have to look my best for you,' she responded as she brushed past me with a toss of the golden hair. Her perfume again instantly infiltrated my nostrils.

'What have you been up to?' I asked tentatively, fearing what the answer maybe.

'Having trouble with my husband,' she replied with disdain.

'Like what?' I said.

'He won't tell me anything about this money situation. I have asked him two or three times to tell me what's going on but all he says is that he doesn't want me to worry my pretty little head about it or some such nonsense. We had a big row about it but he still remains tight lipped on the matter. It's driving me crazy. Sometimes I feel like screaming my head off at him, but so far I haven't.'

For a few moments I tried to think clearly but that was proving difficult as by then she was sat on my settee and kept crossing and uncrossing her legs provocatively in front of me. The short skirt added to the lure and the illusion.

'If you want my serious opinion I think you should let the matter drop,' I said. 'From what I've seen of him I reckon Angus is clever enough and astute enough to get himself out of any sort of mess. And your house and the land must be worth a pretty penny. I would think you've both got that to fall back on if anything serious happened money wise.'

'H'm I don't know,' Carol responded. 'I think there is more to it than just losing some money on our savings. That's why he is not saying much.'

'Well you must do what you think fit Carol,' I said. 'But you could be stirring up a whole hornets nest of trouble for yourself if you pick a fight over it.'

We talked some more around the subject to no obvious conclusion before she said, 'I must go and make the children's tea. Thank you anyway Gareth.' She got up, kissed me firmly on the lips and then was gone out of the front door. Afterwards I stood looking out of the lounge window watching her drive away and across the little narrow bridge up the long driveway to her home. I remained there for sometime thinking about the situation, long after she had gone out of view.

I heard nothing more from her for a while. I was beginning to think the whole matter was a storm in a teacup and that Carol had taken my advice and not raised the subject with her husband. However, as the following week went by I began to notice her absence from around the community.

Normally during the week I would see her or her Range Rover about the village. Either she would call in to see me, or I'd see her or the vehicle in the village store car park, or driving up her driveway towards the big house. But there was no sign of her anywhere. I then made a point when I went down to the village of looking across to the big house at the space where she normally parked the vehicle, but there was no sign of the Range Rover anywhere, although Angus's Mercedes was in view.

That weekend I had intended to do a small fencing job for him in one of his big lower fields. The job only took just over an hour, but afterwards I made a point of calling in on the house to tell Angus I had completed the work and hopefully pick up my fee.

I duly pulled up outside the back door of the house and again noted the absence of Carol's Range Rover. Barking dogs inside retorted their response to my knocking on the back door. Eventually Angus opened up with the four dogs clamouring behind him. When the animals saw me they diverted their attention towards me.

'I've done that little job on the bottom meadow,' I said while fending off the ebullient dogs. 'Ten pounds will do,' I added.

'Well done,' he replied and beckoned me inside. Except for the movements of the animals there was no other sounds about the house.

'Carol and the kids away?' I ventured whilst he searched the kitchen for his wallet.

'Yes they've gone to London for a week,' he said a little tersely. I made no response but thought it a bit strange as I knew it wasn't half term or any school holiday time. We concluded the business and I left pondering on what might have happened between them.

* * * * *

As the activities of these two very different women continued to occupy and fill up my mind I decided to torture myself further by visiting the other one on the Sunday. Again the climb up to the cave was tortuous although the exercise and the freedom seemed to invigorate Bella. When we got close I could again see smoke drifting out of the aperture. Nobody appeared until we were virtually clambering over the front rocks.

Bella ran straight at Mhairi and nearly bowled her over while I was still struggling. 'I wondered if it was you,' she said. 'I thought I heard movement.'

Instantly I could see she had put on weight and that there was a noticeable pregnancy bulge. Bella was far too boisterous for her, I noticed Mhairi tottering a bit and immediately called the dog off. Thankfully she came to heel.

'How are you?' I ventured. 'There's no doubt about the condition you're in now,' I said pointing at the bump of her stomach. Her face had also rounded up quite a bit since my last visit, although the moon and stars were still emblazoned on her forehead. She had however let her dark hair grow longer and it hung attractively around the back of her neck. All the spiky bits were gone which made her much more of a glamorous proposition. In fact with her pregnancy I would say she was positively blooming.

'I'm fine,' she replied, then went into some gobbledy gook. 'Macrinhanish and Skiddlywadles, in fact health wise I've never felt better.'

She offered me a seat on the blankets and rugs, poured me a cup of one of her brews then struggled to sit down beside me.

'Mhairi how are you going to manage up here by yourself when your movements get more restrictive?'

'I've told you I'm fine. There'll be no problems.'

I took a sip of her brew and again it caught in the back of my throat and I had a bit of a choking fit. As she'd done before she laughed at my discomfort.

'Mhairi, most people have a doctor or a nurse in attendance when they have a baby, even if they have the baby at home. You won't be able to cope up here by yourself without some help.'

'I can only repeat what I said to you before on the matter. The animals don't have a doctor or nurse in attendance when they give birth. They have managed by themselves for centuries. Why shouldn't I!'

'Because we are human beings,' I responded. 'Our bodily needs are different.'

'But my bodily needs, as you put it, don't depend on doctors or nurses. I've never consulted a doctor in my life and I don't intend to start now. If I die giving birth or the child dies well that's what happens in nature. Why should I be any different.'

She then went into more of her gobbledigook and I knew I wasn't going to get any further with her on the subject. We talked some more about the weather and the seasons and the animals that lived around her cave before I made to leave. Bella made another fuss of her and I again had to intervene to save Mhairi from being bowled over.

On my way down the mountain the thought of what she was going to go through up there by herself still plagued my mind, especially as I still considered myself responsible for the condition she found herself in. However, it was a clear sky day and when I looked around I could see deer on the top of the mountain above her cave, and, circling high above in the sky two eagles, dipping and floating. 'This a marvellous place to live in,' I said to myself as I scurried on downwards.

* * * * *

I was continuing to worry about the matters relating to these two women when another event addled my mind further. I was on my way to the shop in the village when out of the front entrance of the shop came Carol. We spotted each other instantly.

'Hello stranger?' I said. 'You've been away?'

'Yes I've been away in London,' she replied without elucidating further.

When I looked closely into her face I could see markings around her left eye. They were heavily covered with make-up but from what I could detect underneath it was definitely the remains of a black eye. We talked a bit about London but I could see saying much was difficult for her.

'Would you like to come to the bungalow for a cup of tea?' I said hesitatingly.

At first I thought she was going to refuse but eventually she replied 'That would be nice.'

I told her I had to get a couple of items from the shop but it wouldn't take long. She waited in her car in the shop's car park for me then she drove us to the bungalow. She said very little on the way so I tried to make conversation by talking about the local weather she'd missed.

As soon as I opened the front door and let her into the lounge I immediately spotted the layers of dust on the internal furniture. With her not visiting so regularly recently I had neglected my housekeeping duties.

'If you have a seat I'll put the kettle on. Please take your coat off,' I said.

When I returned from the kitchen with two cups of tea I noticed she was wearing a thick woolly tight fitting sweater and blue slacks.

'You must find it cold up here after London?' I ventured as I sat down opposite her.

'Oh London was so stuffy,' she replied. 'I couldn't wait to get back here to the fresh highland air.'

'Be careful,' I said, 'you might find the tea too hot.'

She rested back in the armchair and I noticed the rise and fall of her breasts. 'Have you been having trouble.' I ventured and pointed at the damaged eye. I could now see now that under the make-up it was slightly puffy below the bottom lid.

She hesitated for a moment before saying, 'It's a lousy story. Do you really want to know about it all?'

'If telling it will help, yes,' I replied. By then Bella had plodded into the lounge and had laid down at my feet.

Carol stretched out for her tea cup and I again noticed the movement of her breasts. I wondered if she was wearing a bra underneath the pullover. 'Well you know about my worries over Angus's investments?' she said, I nodded in response but said nothing. 'I have since discovered that the situation is far worse than I could ever have imagined.' I nodded again and still said nothing, so she continued. 'When I confronted Angus with what I knew, we had a blazing row and he accused me of being an interfering bitch who shouldn't meddle in his affairs.' Another pause while she sipped at her tea. 'As you can imagine that made me even angrier. The row developed. I demanded to know more about what was going on. I made accusations about him risking our children's future. He then went into a rage, like a proper tyrant. I had never seen him like that before. Eventually it came out that he had borrowed money on the security of the house to invest in those funds and he let out that the telephone calls I'd taken were from the bank who had lent the money. They were threatening to foreclose on the loan and take possession of the property to get back their money. I told him he had no right to do that without consulting me as it was my home as well. He told me to mind my own business, then lashed out and hit me in the face with his fist. That night I packed bags for the children and myself and before first light I set off with the two of them for London and our apartment there. I had to come back though because the children are missing schooling.'

'How are things at home now?' I asked.

'Not very good. We're still not speaking except when we have to. It's better when the children are there, but in the day I go out as much as I can when he's in the house. We are not sleeping together.'

'Oh dear,' I said. 'Well you can always escape to the flat in London.'

'I couldn't do that very often with the children needing schooling. I couldn't move them from this school here at the moment and I wonder if he's mortgaged the flat as well. I really don't know what the future holds.'

'Do you think you need to see a solicitor?'

'I don't see the point. At this stage it's not as though he has done anything wrong. As far as I know he hasn't committed adultery or anything like that.'

'Well a solicitor could lodge a second charge in your favour on the house, so that if the bank foreclosed and there was money left in the property you could get some of it when it was sold.'

'I hadn't thought of that, but I don't really want to do that if we can work it out between us before then. We had quite a good marriage until this.'

'Well you've got to look after yourself if there's big trouble. Had you any inkling that something like this might happen?'

'No. I mean when I used to hear him talking on the phone to his business cronies he sounded a completely different man from the guy I married, but I put that down to male bravado and egotism.'

'H'm,' I responded. 'But you must take care and look after yourself. Sometimes men become completely different beings when they get into real financial difficulties. They can often drink too much, which makes them violent. I used to see it in my newspaper reporting days.'

We talked a bit more around the subject, then she made moves to leave.

'Any time you feel like a chat, you're welcome to call,' I said as I helped her on with her coat.

'I am grateful Gareth,' she said and leant into my arms then delivered another passionate kiss.

When she had gone and I was taking Bella on her pre-tea walk I thought more about Carol and her situation. It was difficult to know what to do for the best. I knew I had to be careful, for I was aware that the last thing I should do was to become involved between a man and his wife. That would be just asking for trouble, but Carol had become so kind and helpful to me since my arrival there and the more I saw her the more I became convinced that she had very few friends in the locality except me to download her troubles onto. With her supposed money and situation, and the fact that she was English she was just not the sort of person the locals would bother with. And to make matters worse I was fairly sure she fancied me which made my situation with her even more precarious.

On my return with Bella I met Bob outside his front gate pushing his bicycle. He had been collecting firewood and the timber was straddled across the frame of the bike. Bella made a fuss jumping up at him. He told me that Mhairi had been down to see them and Jessie confirmed that she was pregnant.

CHAPTER SIXTEEN

My mind was still addled when I got inside my bungalow. Then something completely strange occurred. For the first time since I had moved in I could feel Anne's presence in the dwelling around me. When I had first moved in and because of the pain in my heart for her and her disastrous demise, I had tried desperately to blank all thoughts of her from my mind. When I reminisced about her I couldn't cope to do anything much. For a few moments I just stood still and listened for sounds, but there was nothing, just this eerie presence of her sub-consciously being around me, so I called out her name, but there was no reply. Bella must have sensed it for she whimpered, ran over towards me and jumped up at me with her front legs on my chest. Normally by then she would have been barking for her tea. I pushed her off and walked towards the bedroom. Again the room was filled with Anne's being. I looked across to the bed and for an instant I saw her lying under the duvet with her long jet black hair splayed out across the pillow. When I blinked the vision was gone, but I again called out her name. Bella continued to whimper by my side. I walked around the bungalow. Every room was filled with Anne's presence. Bella followed me. Finally I went into the bathroom. Then from behind the glass shower screen I saw the dark outline of a figure move. It was the shape of Anne's body. I again called out her name and stuck my head around the screen, but there was no one there. I moved back to the door and saw the same figure move again behind the screen. I repeated my head movement to look inside it but once more there was no one. I called out her name but no-one appeared and I went to prepare Bella's tea. All the while though I could feel Anne presence was behind me as I did it. Throughout that evening as I watched the television I felt at any moment she was going to open the lounge door and come into the room. It was the same feeling when I went to bed. That night, as I slept, I dreamed continuously of her and all the things we had done together. I had never in my whole life experienced such a demanding sensation. During the following days and weeks I continued to speculate on what had happened, but the sensation never appeared again.

CHAPTER SEVENTEEN

My work life had now settled down again after the trauma of my accident. I was feeling fit and enjoyed the ambience of the surroundings and my work colleagues. Some of the old lags on the squad still continued to treat us incomers as a bit of a joke but those who worked with me were more than happy with the contribution I had made. In a roundabout way their views of my performance did get back to me. On one occasion McIntosh did say to me how pleased he thought the work on the fence line was going. 'That's as tough a bit of ground up there as we have got,' he said. 'Your gang are making faster progress on the project than we thought possible.' And in the hotel bar one evening somebody else said that one of the locals, Danny, who was a foreman 'enjoyed working with me as I liked to get on with the job.'

As always though the weather and its vagaries in that part of the world continued to effect most of the things we tried to do. There were many days in work when we had to sit out a storm in either the work shed by the forestry offices, or in the Land Rover half way up the mountain, as it was too inclement to go outside. I also was still worried and concerned about the two women who had suddenly infiltrated into my life. I have to admit that, apart from work, their problems filled up most of the other spaces in my brain. During that time, for a week or so, we had endured the most violent storms, probably the worst weather since I had been living there. Seventy, eighty mile an hour gales, day and night which were accompanied by continuous lashing rain. It was at times like that when I became particularly worried about Mhairi, considering where she was living and her pregnant condition. How she could continue to survive up there I couldn't imagine. I was often worried, even in my sturdy bungalow, and there were many nights when I wondered if the roof was going to come off. Whenever I saw them I asked Bob and Jessie if they had seen her but they hadn't. 'I'm very worried about her up there in this weather,' I said to them both one day and pointed to the blackened sky.

'A'ch, she's been up there in worse weather than this,' Bob responded.

'But not in her current condition,' I replied.

'Well it's her choice,' Jessie interrupted. 'You're not going to change her now. That's how she's been all her life.'

Regrettably I had to concur with what they were saying. The weather was certainly too bad for me to go up there. There was thick snow on all the peaks above fifteen hundred feet at which height her cave was situated. I might get up there but I probably wouldn't get back down again. I could see from my walks with Bella that I would also never be able to ford the river I had to cross to get on to the mountain, which was more swollen than I had ever seen it before.

All over the region trees were down blocking many roads and as a working gang we were often called out to assist in the clearing of them. Around the village rivers and streams were rising faster than even some of the locals could remember. In some places they were going over their banks and flooding across the roads. The loch was certainly higher up than I had seen it in all my time there.

When I got home from work that evening, although we hadn't been up to the fencing line all day, my clothes were still soaked from just going in and out of the shed near the forestry offices on odd jobs throughout the day. So it wasn't worth changing to take Bella out, but when I did we didn't stay out long as she didn't seem to want to be out in that weather either. Once back inside we both soon settled down to eat our teas as it began to get dark outside.

As I was clearing away the dishes I heard a rapping noise on my front door. I tried looking out the front window but could see nothing but the lashing rain. When I opened up the door I could see Carol standing outside, dripping water profusely.

'Good gosh, come in out of that quickly please,' I hastened to say.

Without saying a word she stepped inside and removed her dripping rain jacket while she was still in the front porch way. 'I'll hang this here,' she said pointing towards a coat hook on the adjacent inside wall, then we both walked into the lounge.

'What on earth are you doing out on a night like this?' I ventured.

'Oh, I had to take the kids to a school thing at Salen. If I had known the roads and the weather were so awful I wouldn't have done so, but they're there now. They can stay with one of my friends for the night. I'm not going back for them in this, but that's not the worst of it. When I tried to get home down our driveway it looks to me that our bridge is either down or collapsing. I didn't dare try the Range Rover on it in case it all collapsed with me on board.'

'Oh Gosh,' I responded. 'We'd better go and take a look.'

I put on all my forestry waterproof gear. 'You'd better wait here,' I added.

'No way. I'll come with you,' she said. I gave her a spare pair of my waterproof trousers and she reverted to the waterproof jacket she was wearing when she'd arrived. I grabbed a flashlight torch from the kitchen windowsill and we went outside.

I almost wish we hadn't. The rain was coming down so hard that even with the outside light on we couldn't see the front gate. We decided not to risk the Range Rover. 'I wouldn't want that sliding off the road and getting stuck in the ditch,' I said, so we walked towards the bridge. It was only sixty or seventy yards away, but just going that far was hard enough. The road itself was more like the river. Regularly the flowing water reached the top of my boots and we both had to jump over the deeper parts of it to make progress. Needless to say the sky above was black as ink which made seeing anything difficult. My bungalow outside light now seemed a long way off and the beam my torch gave out was almost useless.

However, somehow we both made it to the bridge. The rushing sound of the river cascading downstream towards the loch made talking difficult, so we made do with mostly sign language. After shining my torch repeatedly on various parts of the bridge's structure it appeared that one of the walls protecting it from the river's down flow had completely collapsed. No way in that storm and on that night could I allow Carol to attempt crossing it, either on foot or by any vehicle. It was just far too dangerous. I made attempts by voice and with sign language to illustrate my point. By her nodding head I could see that she more or less agreed with my findings.

I motioned for us to go back to my bungalow. This was even harder as to a certain extent we were fighting to walk upstream. Inside my front porch we both had to take deep breaths before we had the energy to remove our waterproof garments. We needed to hold onto each other whilst we did so.

I grabbed clean towels for both of us and in the lounge area we both tried to dry off. I turned up the fire as we were both shivering. We had to tip water from our shoes into the kitchen sink and we padded around in bare feet.

'I really ought to get in touch somehow with Angus,' she said next. 'Despite our current differences he'll be worried sick, particularly about the children.'

I reminded her that I didn't have a phone. 'I shall have to try to get over there to see him then,' she responded.

'No way will I let you try and cross that bridge. You'll kill yourself and that will be no use to anybody.'

We discussed any other way we could get to her house, but without climbing and traipsing across half a mountain there wasn't, but in that weather, that was also out the question. Then I suddenly remembered that Bob and Jessie had a phone. It would mean going back up the rain soaked road to their cottage, but she could at least phone Angus from there.

We therefore had to re-dress into our soaking wet clothes and make our way up the tide-like road the two hundred yards or so to their place. Within minutes we were as wet as we'd been before. It took several minutes rapping on their front door to bring them to answer it. When they did however they were both shocked to see us standing there in that condition. I explained our predicament. 'Of course come in,' Jessie said. Carol and I both removed our saturated shoes before we went in beyond the front porch.

Bob pointed to the phone on the hall table and Carol set about phoning her home number. I walked into the lounge with the other two and was immediately struck, in my warm wet clothes, by the heat from their wood fire going full blast in the hearth. I apologised for dripping water on their carpet, but didn't dare remove it as I knew it would create even more water.

'Ach you don't have to worry about that,' Jessie said. 'When they've been sick we've had the lambs in here.'

In the hall I could hear Carol talking animatedly to her husband on the phone. 'I'll have to spend the night with a friend,' I heard her say. I detected his voice on the other end of the line but couldn't make out his reply. Within a few more moments she had rung off and joined us in the lounge.

'I apologise for that,' she said to them both, 'but thank you. I left some money for the call.'

'Och you didn't have to do that,' Bob responded.

'Yes I did and I thank you again,' she replied.

Carol and I made our further apologies and then left Bob and Jessie to get on with watching their programme on the TV. On my way out I noticed she had left a five pound note on the hall table which in those days could have bought a meal out for two in the Highlands.

Once more we needed to wade down the flooded road to my bungalow. Fortunately this time the howling gale was at our backs, although the torrential rain was still sweeping across the blackened sky. When we reached the front gate, I said to her, 'You can't go far in this.'

'I thought I'd spend the night in the hotel,' she said.

'Don't be stupid,' I responded quickly. 'You'll probably get washed away going back down the road and you don't know if the road bridge across to the village is damaged just like yours. Then you'd be unable to get to the hotel and it will all have been a waste of time. You'll have to spend the night at my place.' For a moment we just stood and looked at each other.

'Do you trust me,' Carol retorted.

'Not for one moment,' I replied, 'but I'm prepared to risk it and go through whatever pain it takes.'

For a moment in the beam of my outside light I could see her sharp blue eyes flash at me, then she burst into laughter. With the gale still blowing it took the two of us to struggle to close the five barred gate, then we both went inside the bungalow to be greeted by a whimpering and leaping Bella.

Once I had removed my boots and my outer jacket I went to stoke up the wood fire in the lounge and switch on all the electric fires in the other rooms. We then continued to dry ourselves off again with the already wet towels.

'I'm going to have to change out of all of this Gareth,' she said, pointing at her body. 'If I don't remove my bra and pants I'm going to get pneumonia, they're soaked right through.'

I ushered her towards the bathroom, reached for another dry towel from the airing cupboard then closed the door when she was inside. In my bedroom I removed all my clothes and replaced them with dry ones. Afterwards I fished around in my wardrobe for a shirt and some shorts which she could possibly try to put on. Then I knocked on the bathroom door. 'Here try these,' I said. When she opened the door fractionally I handed them inside. She'd hid behind the door. 'Have a shower if you like,' I added, 'the water is hot.' She closed the door and from what I could hear she availed herself of that facility.

Whilst I was searching around in my depleted larder in the kitchen cupboard for something I could cook which we could both eat, she appeared in the doorway, with the towel wrapped around her head, and wearing one of my summer t-shirts and shorts. The sight was amazing, she could have been on a beach in the Caribbean. I could tell she had no bra on, but I tried to concentrate on practicalities in hand.

'I'm afraid the best I can offer is a steak and kidney pie, which is tinned, and some potatoes and carrots?'

'Sounds good to me. Do you want me to help?'

'No. You're my guest. In the sideboard is half a bottle of opened red wine and some glasses. Pour yourself a large one and I'll have the same.'

She did as instructed and returned with the drinks. 'Now you go and thaw out by the fire in the lounge. You can watch the TV if you like. If I don't burn all of this I'll call you when it is ready.'

'Yes sir! Cheers,' she added, giggling. We toasted each other and then she went off to the lounge.

We both managed to eat what I had prepared. 'You're quite domesticated aren't you,' she said afterwards. We were both by then chewing on an apple.

'When you live on your own you have to be,' I replied. 'Although it's not always as posh as this,' I said pointing at the tablecloth. Afterwards I washed up and she wiped. I made us both a cup of coffee which we took into the, by then, very warm lounge.

'Now TV or music?' I asked.

'Music, if that's OK with you.'

From my record collection I handed her a selection of LPs and she chose one by Carol King. Then we sat out the rest of the evening side by side on the sofa listening to the music and talking. To keep my hands off her scantily clad body and legs was a real struggle.

When it got to about ten o'clock, I said, 'I'm afraid I am going have to think about bed now as I have to be up at six in the morning to get myself ready for work.'

'Oh dear, poor you.'

'That's the way it is I'm afraid. I'll sleep in the spare room. You can have my bed as it's bigger and more comfortable.'

'By myself?'

'I think it might be best,' I responded.

'Best for who?'

I made no reply and we began to organise ourselves with the sleeping arrangements. Before she went into my bedroom she said, 'As I haven't my nightie with me I'll sleep in the nude.' I hurried for the other bedroom quickly.

* * * * *

With those thoughts still going around in my head I somehow managed to drift off to sleep. I was awoken about an hour or so later by the feeling of Carol's naked body crawling in alongside me. 'I was too cold and lonely in there by myself,' she said while her hands roamed all over me. I was instantly sexually aroused and my hands began to fondle her breasts. They were beautiful.

'What about your husband?'

'Oh he and I haven't had sex for months,' she replied. 'I think he has lost interest in me anyway.'

'Well if we are going to spend the night together we'd better go back to my room, the bed's bigger and more comfortable.'

So that's what we did. Instantly I began to make love to her and by her moans and yelps I could tell she was thoroughly enjoying it. Often she called out for 'more please.' We continued in that manner for most of the night. Sometimes she would be on top of me and then it would be the other way round. In between we would sleep for perhaps half an hour before I would again feel her hands about me. I lost count of the number of times we did it. Most of the night I could still hear the gale howling away outside.

Sometime around dawn I could again felt her turn towards me. I looked across at the bedside clock which showed it was five thirty. 'Now I'm going make love to you so you have something nice to think about while you are at work. Gareth that is the best nights sex I have ever had. I want to be your mistress please.'

While I was lying stretched out I noticed that the gale had stopped blowing outside. When I eventually got up and drew back the curtain I saw that it had stopped raining as well.

I quickly washed, threw on some clothes and went to the front door. It had definitely stopped raining and the gale had ceased as well. Outside the front door still stood the Range Rover. I could see beyond that the road was relatively clear although there were fallen small branches strewn everywhere. I went down to the front gate and could see that the road itself was drivable.

I went back inside where Carol was in the process of getting dressed. I could only admire the figure I'd held in my arms most of the night. I put my arms around her shoulders and we kissed passionately.

'That was a great night,' I said when I came up for air.

'It was indeed,' she replied. 'When can we do it again?'

I chuckled. 'I think we better move your car before the village wakes up and realises you've spent the night here. If the forestry lads see it when they pick me up at half seven I'll never live it down.'

She agreed. I said I would move it but she insisted that now the road was clear that she was quite capable of doing it herself. She said she would wait at the loch side for half an hour then when enough time had elapsed she would drive down to Salen to pick up her kids. From there she would phone Angus and tell him she spent the night with a friend in the village. When she was gone my head was still in a spin as I prepared my breakfast. I learnt later that at first light Angus had organised some men to come repair their bridge.

CHAPTER EIGHTEEN

So that night changed my life completely. As Carol had requested we became permanent lovers. Usually we got together for a couple of hours at the weekend when Angus had taken the children off on a jaunt for most of the day. I normally walked to their house, but always carried with me some fencing tool or some such implement to make it look as though I was going there to do some work. I never took the van and she never came to my place except to bring me some shopping with kids on board in the Range Rover after school, as she had done for the past few months, but she never stopped long. We didn't want the villagers to see her at my place for any length of time. Our love making continued in its frenetic manner on a large bed in one of the old guest rooms in the roof space of her big house. You could regularly hear the rain clattering on the roof.

From what she told me her relationship with Angus had deteriorated further. By all accounts his drinking habits had increased, so most of the time she tried to keep out of his way, as when they were around each other it usually developed into a big argument. She admitted that as a pair neither of them would back down so that usually made things worse. She was also becoming increasingly worried about their financial situation as she could regularly hear him on the phone arguing with his creditors or whoever and there was increasing mail obviously on the same subject. She didn't open any of it though, or that would have made his temper worse, but she could see from the envelopes who they were from. During that time I had no opportunity to see Mhairi but I did think about her often, and worry. Nobody had seen her around anywhere. My work continued to be enjoyable and with my new found love life I guess I possessed more zest.

At one of our trysts Carol told me that during that week they had received a visit from three men who she guessed were bankers.

She wasn't allowed into the room during their meeting with Angus but from what she could hear standing outside the door, listening to them, was what they were discussing was foreclosing on their loan and threatening to take possession of the property. Angus of course didn't tell her any of this but she said to me that she was desperately worried particularly for the children.

'I suppose you could always take them to London and live in the flat?' I said.

'But I don't want take them away from here and their school,' she said spreading her arms out wide. 'And how would they cope in London?'

'Well many kids have to.' I replied. 'Children at that age are adaptable. When I was about four my parents moved from a seaside town in North Wales to Cardiff. That was a pretty big culture shock, I can tell you.'

'I don't know,' she responded. 'The apartment may be in hock to the banks as well.'

'Well I mentioned before that perhaps you should see a solicitor of your own. At least he would tell where you stood legally in all of this.'

'H'm,' she replied.

Our joint lives continued in that manner for another week or two, but from our regular conversations I gathered that matters between Angus and Carol had continued to deteriorate.

Then one day in the afternoon when I had got home from work there was a hammering on my front door. I looked out of the front window and could see Carol standing outside with the children in the Range Rover in the front driveway. It was about her normal time of calling but she looked most agitated and worried and I quickly let her in.

'I'm afraid I'm in a hell of a state,' were her first words.

'What's the trouble?' I replied.

'It's Angus. He's not returned all night and now not all day. I don't know what to think.'

'Maybe he's gone to Glasgow or London to sort out his finances?'

'But if he's done that he always phones at some time or another. Even when we've been arguing he likes to speak to the kids before they go to bed. I've phoned the apartment in London and there's no reply. I've phoned some of his friends who I know and they haven't seen him.'

'H'm,' I responded. 'Would you like a drink or something? Calm you down.'

'No thanks. I've got to get the kids tea. Gareth I just don't know what to do.'

'I think you should go home with the children and see to them. You never know he may have just got stuck late in a meeting and will soon be home. If there is no change by this time tomorrow we'll have to think of what to do next.'

'I guess you're right,' she said. She reached for her handkerchief and began to sob. I pulled her into my arms and hugged her and kissed her.

'I'm sorry for you to see me like this,' she said.

We hugged some more. She dried her eyes then she was gone. I stood at my front door and watched her drive away. Afterwards I thought a lot about her situation and hoped I hadn't aggravated it.

Then the next day at about the same time she returned again to my bungalow, looking even more distraught. 'He has not returned,' she said as she entered in through the front door. That day she looked very strained. She had obviously also been crying. 'I've tried ringing the apartment in London on and off all day but there's still no reply. I even rang at two clock this morning in case he had got back in late from somewhere, but nothing. Gareth I just don't know what to do?'

'How long is it now?' I asked.

'Three days,' she replied almost screaming out the words.

'I think we ought to report it to the police then. He is now a missing person.'

'Do you think I am being silly?'

'Of course not. I'll come with you, I know Jack Banyard.'

'You're very kind to me.'

I made no reply to that, changed into some slightly more respectable clothes, settled Bella into her bed in the kitchen, which she undertook with a bored 'humph' and then we drove off down to the village in the Range Rover, with the kids sitting on the back seats.

As soon as we entered the small police station Jack Banyard came out from the back room to the front counter to see us. I explained to him that I was a friend of both Angus and Carol and that I often did fencing work and the like for them and then explained the current problem to him. He listened intently then asked us both to sit in chairs opposite the desk while he sat in one behind the desk. He took out a large form from one of the desk drawers and then directed his attention to Carol. Slowly and methodically he asked her questions about their personal details and a résumé of the current events. Carol answered them clearly and bravely. She even told him about the recent financial problem. He wrote all her answers down on the form.

'Well I'll have to tell my people at Fort William,' he said when he had finished his questions. 'They will almost certainly want to come over and see you,' he said to Carol. 'They will also probably want to search your house and the grounds as well. Are you happy with that?'

She nodded her head in agreement but said nothing.

'Ok,' he responded. 'Either I or they will phone when they're coming. I have your phone number here,' he said pointing to the form. 'Will the children be all right?'

'If it's in the day time they will be in school. If it's going to be a problem at night they can go and stay with a friend,' she replied.

'OK, good,' Banyard said and got up out of his chair, we did likewise. We all made our farewells and Carol and I left to drive to the bridge across the river to her house where I got out.

'Gareth I am most grateful,' she said as I stood outside the door of the Range Rover.

'No problem,' I said, 'that's what friends are for.' I waved into the back to the kids and she drove off over the repaired bridge towards her house. I could see there were no lights on inside at that moment.

* * * * *

Later on that evening when I took Bella out for her last walk, we went as far as the river bridge that crossed to Carol's house. From there I had a clear view of her dwelling. Some of the lights were on, but the only car I could see in the parking area was her Range Rover. I went back to my bed wondering.

I heard nothing more on the matter until the following afternoon when Carol called on me at her usual time after school. On letting her in I asked, 'How are things going?'

'Oh not so good,' she replied. I helped her off with her coat, kissed her on the lips and guided her through to the lounge, where she sat on the sofa. I sat next to her. She looked more strained than on the previous day. 'Still no sign of him,' she then said.

'Have the police been?'

'Oh my God yes. It was like the third degree. Five of them, plus a sniffer dog. My dogs went mad. I had to shut them in the bathroom. Banyard also came along as well. I guess he guided them here, although he only came as far as the front door when I let them in. Three of them interviewed me, one a woman, while the other two and the dog searched the house. They even went into the attic. They were inside for about an hour and a half, they took down my life's history and all about the current problems, then they all went outside except the woman who stayed with me trying to offer words of comfort. I could see them going in and out of all the outbuildings and the one with the dog searching across the fields. After about another hour and a half they came inside and said that as far as they could see they could find no trace of Angus. 'They told me that they would have to extend their search further afield, but they would be in touch daily.'

For a couple of days after that, on school days, after picking up the kids, Carol would still come to visit me with some food shopping about the usual time after my work day was over. She never stayed long. We didn't indulge in any sexual intercourse. There was still no news of Angus and each day she looked more strained and worried.

'Are you all right for money?' I ventured one day.

'At the moment, yes thankfully. There is still money in our Midland account, which is my housekeeping, etc. account and the dividends that fund it are still coming in. They are from some of our long standing investments and Angus doesn't seem to have messed about with those yet.'

'Good,' I responded and soon afterwards she left.

At the weekend, on the Saturday morning, I walked across to her house carrying some fencing tools as camouflage for the purpose of my visit. She let me in. I was greeted by the dogs. The two kids were playing in the kitchen. After hellos all round she took me through to their large impressive lounge and closed the door, then we engaged in a more passionate kiss and embrace, although we both knew there could be no real sexual hanky panky with the children around. She was wearing a black t-shirt, tight blue jeans, but no socks or shoes. Her blonde hair was tied up in a tight bun and she still looked very strained.

'Any news?' was my first real question.

'Nothing,' she replied.

'Have the police been in touch.'

'Oh yes, every day to report that as yet they have discovered nothing. Everybody they contact who I know he knew says they have heard or seen nothing of him either. A few of them have rung me up to commiserate, but I told them that there was nothing they can really do at the moment, as I am comfortable and can cope by myself here,' she said waving her arm around the room. 'And honestly I think I'm better by myself. And I've always got you if I'm desperate,' she smiled.

We both laughed. 'Well you must be pretty desperate,' I responded. We both laughed some more. That was the first time in days I'd seen her smile properly.

I stayed for another half hour to talk things through. She told me she didn't really need anything except me, then after saying goodbye to the kids I left.

I was still worried about them both, for despite what Carol had moaned about Angus, I had found him to be a good guy and I had no real truck with him. He had been very generous to me with payment for the work I had done and out in the fields we had shared a few manly laughs. Over the weekend, in my mind, I tried to go over the possible scenarios of what may have happened with him. Some were quite galling. Carol had told me that he hadn't taken with him any extra clothes or anything like that. She said he'd obviously taken his wallet and cheque book and his car but that was about it.

Nothing further happened until the Monday. I had gone to work at seven thirty in the morning and at that time everything looked quiet over at their house. However when the Forestry Land Rover dropped me at home, after work, I looked across there and could see two police cars and Jack Banyard's smaller one outside. I dashed inside my bungalow changed into cleaner clothes and got into my van and drove over there.

I rapped on the back door and heard the dogs bark. Jack Banyard answered it. He stepped outside. 'I'm afraid there's bad news,' he said.

'Oh my God what?' I replied.

'We've found Mr McLeod today.'

'Where?'

'In his car in the old disused quarry a mile off the Salen road. I'm afraid he's dead. There was a tube attached to the car's exhaust, which had been inserted into a tiny gap in one of the car's windows. Alongside Mr McLeod on the passenger seat were two empty bottles of whisky. Everything points to him having taken his own life. He has been taken to Fort William for an autopsy.'

'Oh my Lord. I did wonder if that was a possibility,' I said. 'How's Carol?'

'Distraught as you can imagine.'

'Is it possible to see her?'

He hesitated before replying. 'Hang on here a minute I'll go and see if that's OK. I'll shut the door or the dogs might get out.' With that he was gone inside.

He was back within a few minutes. 'That's OK,' he said. 'Come in we've put the dogs in the downstairs bathroom. Obviously Mrs McLeod is in a bad state.'

I wiped my feet on the doormat. When inside, Banyard closed the door behind me. 'They're all in the lounge' he said. 'The chief inspector is in there with her and a lady policewoman.' He pointed the way there.

In the lounge they were all seated. Carol was clutching a handkerchief and was obviously sobbing. When she saw me she got out of her seat and came across the room towards me. We hugged and I kissed her on the forehead.

'I'm so sorry,' I said as we hugged, then we both moved towards adjacent chairs. 'My name is Gareth Rees, a friend and neighbour from across the road,' I said to the two police people who remained on the settee.

'This is Inspector Neville and policewoman McCullough from Fort William,' Banyard said. The three us nodded at each other and I sat down.

'Where are the kids?' I said to Carol.

'My friend at Salen has picked them up. They are going stay down there for a few days. They all go to the same school anyway. I've told them that their Dad is very ill and has had to go into hospital'.

'Good. Well done.'

We all talked some more about the prior problems particularly relating to Angus' financial troubles. Carol told them that I knew about some of it and that I was trying to find someone financially capable of helping her. They wanted to know my full postal address. I told them I didn't have a phone but that Jack Banyard knew how to contact me if needed. I told them I worked for the forestry commission locally. They wanted to know how long I had been doing that, how long I'd lived up there and what work I'd done down south.

In all, the four of us were together about another hour before they made moves to leave.

'What about the car?' I asked. 'Is it driveable?'

'Yes, we think so,' Banyard said. 'At the moment forensics are looking at it but then it should be moveable, although I don't think there will be any petrol left in at as I think Mr McLeod left the engine running whilst he died.' Carol sobbed at that.

'Can I go down and pick it up when it's all clear?'

'Yes please,' Carol interrupted

They all agreed. 'I'll drive you down there and help with that,' Banyard said.

Then we shook hands and they made to leave. On his way out through the door Neville said he would send for some trauma help for Carol and added that if she was going to leave the house for any prolonged period, like overnight, she was to let Banyard know. We all agreed to that.

When they'd gone Carol said she would make us both some coffee. She let the dogs out of the bathroom and they bounded all over us while sniffing around the house where the visitors had been. We sat in the kitchen and talked while we drank it.

'Gareth I hope I haven't caused all this by my nagging?' she said and sobbed a bit more.

'I don't see how when he wouldn't tell you anything. Anyway you don't know yet what real financial trouble he was in.'

'I expect I'll soon find out,' she said.

Within a short while she received a telephone call from a woman who said she was a trauma councillor and was at the village police station with Banyard and asked if it was all right to come up and see her. Carol agreed. Within ten minutes she and Banyard were knocking on the front door. Inside he introduced her as Susan Cartwright. She was tall, dark haired and I guess in her middle thirties.

'I think Mrs Cartwright will want to be alone with Mrs McLeod for a while,' Banyard said. He and I went off towards the kitchen.

'I'd better go home and get myself something to eat and see to the dog,' I said. 'I came over here straight from work when I saw the police cars. Tell Carol I will be back later on to see if she needs anything.' He said he would do that.

He said, 'By tomorrow I think Mr McLeod's car will be ready to pick up.'

'Well I have to go to work first,' I replied. 'But after four thirty I should be OK to go.'

'Good. I'll pick you up after that then. I'll organise some petrol,' he said. I then left for my bungalow and Bella.

That evening, when it was dark I walked across to the big house. Carol let me in through the front door. In the hallway she collapsed into my arms and we hugged and kissed for some time. While we did so the four big red setters kept jumping up at us. Eventually we made our way through to the lounge and sat beside each other. She had lit a log fire in the hearth which made the big room warm.

'How did it go with Susan Cartwright?' I asked.

'Oh, OK. She was quite helpful really. She asked if I wanted someone to stay with me for the night or if I wanted to go and stay with anybody else. I told her no. I would be better here by myself and I've got the dogs and a phone. She said she would come back and see me in the daytime tomorrow. But will you stay with me for the night, please Gareth?'

'Of course I will.'

So that's what we did. We slept together in a big double bed in one of the guest rooms. We did have sex, but it was more of a comforting exercise rather than sexual indulgence. She cried through most of it and through most of the night. I made sure to leave before it got light as I had to see to Bella and my breakfast before the seven thirty forestry Land Rover would pick me up for work.

Later in the day, after work I saw Banyard's police car pull up outside my front door. I had changed out of my forestry gear and was ready to go. 'I've got some petrol,' he said as I got in the front seat and sat alongside him. It transpired that he'd brought with him a two gallon plastic tank full of petrol in the boot of his car. We drove to the quarry.

It was certainly an eerie and isolated spot down a narrow and disused track, well off the Salen road. In fact up until then I didn't even know it existed. The quarry itself was like a rocky amphitheatre with rocks lying around everywhere. We could see Angus' Mercedes parked in the middle. I thought that if you were going to do the deed that this was certainly the place to do it. Banyard had with him the car's keys. First we lifted up the bonnet and checked the oil and water levels which seemed OK. Then we walked around to look at tyres which all looked perfectly drivable. Between us we poured the petrol via a funnel into the car's tank.

'Let's give it a go,' Banyard said and handed me the keys. 'You'll probably have to crank it a few times to pump the petrol through to the engine,' he added.

He was right. It took about a dozen goes before the engine burst into life. I let it run on half throttle for some minutes to make sure it didn't stall.

'You'd better drive it round here slowly first,' Banyard said. 'Check the brakes and clutch work before we go on the road.'

I did that. It was hard going trying to avoid the rocks that were strewn all over the place. Eventually I pulled up alongside him and said. 'It seems OK to me.'

'Right,' he responded. 'Take it slowly though it's a big car to drive. I'll follow on behind you.'

He did that right up to Carol's front door where she was waiting. He then turned his car round, wound down the window and said, 'I'll leave you now.' I gave him the thumbs up and we watched him drive back down the driveway. Then I suddenly remembered I hadn't paid him for the petrol. I made a mental note to drop the money into the police station next day.

Carol and I kissed passionately in the hallway, then went through into the lounge. 'The car's OK,' I said and handed her the keys.

'Thanks for that,' she replied.

'How have you been today?' I asked.

'Pretty lousy. I still blame myself for this. Susan Cartwright has been. She was quite helpful again.'

'Good,' I responded. 'You mustn't blame yourself that's not fair. You saw what state Angus was in with his drinking and problems. That is how it affects some men. If they get into financial trouble it goes against their ego and their pride. And occasionally that's how they react. I've seen it before when I worked as a reporter.'

I was not going to stay the night as Angus's brother and family were coming down to stay and arrange the funeral, which was to take place on the following Monday at the local church. I kept well away from the house until after they had gone in the middle of that week. Before the funeral there was an inquest which I didn't attend, but Carol and his brother did. Carol found it all quite harrowing and told me that the Procurator Fiscal decided that, unfortunately, the only verdict he could come to was that Angus had taken his own life due to the financial pressures he was under. He did however express his sorrow to Carol and 'her young family.' The children did not attend. I did however attend the church service and sat at the back, and the burial in the adjacent graveyard, as did most of the villagers, which was the tradition in those parts. There was a wake at the hotel afterwards but I didn't go to that.

Rachel and Cameron, Carol's two children, didn't attend the funeral and didn't in fact return to their home until after the funeral and Angus's family had left. Then Carol told them that their father had died with a bad illness in hospital at Fort William.

CHAPTER NINETEEN

And so gradually our lives returned to some sort of normality. Carol and I continued with our sexual liaisons but we were careful to do it when the children were not there, like when they had to attend a school function or stayed overnight with their friends in Salen. Even though our get togethers were less frequent they remained sexually satisfying. I guess an absence or maybe abstinence makes the heart grow fonder.

In work I continued to work flat out and around Carol's house there were odd repair jobs to do at the weekend. So all in all when I got into my own bed at night I was bushed and slept like a log. Still no news or sight of Mhairi.

Each day though further details of Angus' serious financial problems gradually came to light. One day she asked me to accompany her to Fort William to meet up with his solicitors. To do so I needed to take an afternoon off work. She drove us over there in her Range Rover, where I was introduced to Hamish Allan in his cramped paper and file strewn office. She told him I was a friend who was helping her as I used to be a financial journalist in South Wales, which was of course a bit of a white lie. Anyway he seemed happy with that.

When we'd all sat down he picked up a large full brown file which was obviously Angus' folder. He began by saying that the problems were pretty serious. Firstly one of the Banks had an order for possession on her home. A second Bank also had what's called a second charge on the property which meant that if the first Bank repossessed, the second Bank would have next claim on any money that was left after a forced sale. Carol and I just looked at each other. Allan said that he had so far managed to stall the possession order with the first Bank because of Angus' death, but that they would not hold off for ever as their debt was mounting due to the accumulating interest.

Then he started to reveal the figures involved which were quite frightening. The first Bank were owed over three hundred thousand pounds which in those days was an astronomical amount of money. The second Bank were owed the best part of two hundred thousand pounds. There were other debts as well but nothing like those figures.

'I just don't know what he thought he was doing,' Carol interjected.

I interrupted. 'I've said to Mrs McLeod that she also should lodge a charge on the property as she is not a co-owner. At least that way if there is any money left over at the end she may get some of it. Can you arrange that?' I said to Allan.

'Yes I can do that,' he replied.

Then we came to what Angus had done with the money. From a schedule he read out nearly half a million pounds originally had been invested in a fund called Cambrian New Earth Investment Fund which had collapsed into bankruptcy three months ago.

'Why would he do such a stupid thing?' Carol responded.

'I can't say,' Allan replied. 'Sometimes people get coerced into what the financial salesmen are trying to sell them. Some of these funds, for a short while, have a very good track record, but usually that is only a fleeting gain. I'm afraid these guys are persuasive and people do get taken in by it.'

'I wish I'd known about it,' Carol said. Allan just shook his head in response.

'So where do we go from here?' I asked.

'Well, I'll try and stay off the possession proceedings for as long as I can because of Mrs McLeod's and her children's situation, but I can't promise that will hold out for long. Under the law the Banks are entitled to their money one way or another,' Allan said in his morbid Scottish tones.

'Do we know the name of the Financial Advisor who dealt with all of Angus's money?' I asked.

Allan consulted his file.

'From what I can see the man's name is Edward Sharpe,' he replied. 'He seems to be based in Glasgow and is employed by the firm we've mentioned.'

Again Carol and I looked across at each other. With subsequent events it was a name I was unlikely to forget.

'Did Angus have any pension provisions?' I asked Allan.

Again he checked the file. 'From what I can see,' he replied, 'Mr McLeod cashed in all his pension fund to invest in the Cambrian Investment fund.'

Carol and I again just looked at each other and shook our heads in amazement.

We talked some more then I asked. 'Is Mrs McLeod entitled to any social security help?'

'Depends on what other income she has,' Allan replied. 'You're perfectly entitled to apply for help.'

Eventually we left his office wondering where the hell we went from there with this matter. As we were in town we called in at the local Social Security office. They asked a lot of questions and filled in pages of forms and then said they would be in touch.

Carol drove us both home and I commiserated with her all the way there.

Over the next few days I tried to think of the best next course of action to try and help her. One day, while I was working in the mountains, I remembered my old working colleague Charles Watson. Some of my visits to see Carol were on a Saturday morning to attend to the odd jobs around the house and cut some firewood for her to last the week. The kids were usually at the house as well so there was no way we could get involved in any sexual hanky panky. But of course I knew Carol had a telephone there from which I could ring Watson.

When I suggested it to her she replied, 'Of course you can use the phone. It's for my benefit anyway.'

'Good, I'll do it now, if I can, before he goes out.' I dialled his number. He answered.

After I reminded him of who I was he replied, 'I'm still waiting for that bottle of Highland Malt.'

'You'll get it. I haven't been down there since.' Then I reminded him of our problem and our latest discoveries relating to it.

After a few minutes I told him about the Cambrian fund, the amount Angus had invested and its subsequent fall into bankruptcy. I also asked him if he could find out anything about the financial salesman Edward Sharpe, who was based in Glasgow.

Watson said he'd look into it. I said I would ring him back again in two hours. He agreed to that. While I waited I went outside to chop some firewood. There were plenty of wind blows (fallen timber) around the estate for those purposes. The activity soon got me warm.

When I went inside the house again with the freshly cut wood Carol made me a cup of coffee and we talked some more about all her problems. After just over two hours had elapsed I phoned back Watson.

'Seems like a right shenanigans with this lot,' were his first words.

'Let me know the worst,' I responded.

'This Cambrian fund you mentioned went bust about four months ago. This guy Sharpe, you also mentioned, appears to be a right crook. Despite McLeod's losses he will have earned substantial commission on the investments, which normally he will still keep despite the fund going into liquidation. Because he's based in Glasgow I can't find much more about him. You'll have to do that locally. But from past experience I don't think McLeod's wife will get any of the money back.'

He ended up commiserating about her situation. 'I'm afraid this happens a lot with these investment funds nowadays. On paper and on past performance they look so attractive but there are no scruples in the business at all.' We talked some more then he finished by saying,

'Don't forget the whisky!'

'I won't,' I replied.

I went back into the kitchen and broke all the news to Carol. As I did so I watched her face contort into pain.

'What am I and the children going to do if we are evicted?' she said and reached for her handkerchief, which was tucked inside her sleeve. I could see it had had a lot of use recently.

'I think we'd better talk to Allan again on Monday. We forgot to ask him about the flat and I want to ask him to find out what he can about this guy Sharpe. I will come straight over after work on Monday and we'll phone him then, he should be there until at least five o'clock.'

So that's what we did. The Forestry Land Rover dropped me at my front gate at about four o' clock. I took Bella around the garden, dished out her tea for her in the kitchen, got out of my Forestry togs, had a quick shower, changed into some more respectable clothes and then drove over to the big house.

Carol had returned from picking up the kids from school. She was making them some tea and she made me a cup of coffee and toast with honey on it. I needed that after the days work. When I'd finished eating I phoned Allan and she stood by my side while I talked to him.

When Allan answered I told him that Carol was standing alongside me. Firstly I told him some of the information Charles Watson had told me.

'I do wish my clients would come and consult me before investing this type of money into such schemes. OK, occasionally we all have a flutter and invest a few grand on a hunch but not all our worldly wealth. That's crazy. As well as investing all his pension fund in this scheme, I mean he's borrowed these large amounts of money from these banks on the security of his homes. Again, crazy.'

I could only agree with him. 'What about the flat in London?' I asked. 'Is there a bank loan on that with an order for possession on it as well?'

'There is a big bank loan on that yes, with another bank, but as yet no order for possession. They have been writing to him about it though, and they could start on that procedure at any moment.'

'I was thinking, that if the bank repossesses the property here in Scotland, Mrs McLeod and the children could go and live there in London, for a while anyway.'

'Well I will do my best to forestall both situations but the matter is really up to the banks. Whatever I may say the decision is almost entirely in their hands. Of course if Mrs McLeod and the children are homeless the local authority here have a duty to re-house them.'

We then went on to discuss this shit Edward Sharpe. Watson said he didn't know him and had never dealt with him but he would make enquiries with the Law Society and the like in Glasgow to see if they knew anything about him. He said he would need a few days to deal with it. I said I would phone him again on Thursday after work. He agreed to that.

So again on the Thursday I followed the same procedure and went across the river to Carol's house. She had got some shopping in for me and again made me some coffee, this time accompanied by some hot buttered crumpets. They were delicious. By then she had also received some mail from the Social Security in Fort William. They had come to no firm conclusions on her situation but did ask more questions which made it look hopeful. During the week she had also seen Susan Cartwright again and confirmed that she had once more been helpful.

I duly phoned Allan. 'This man Sharpe looks a complete scoundrel to me,' were his first words. 'Sharpe is the right word to describe him.' Allan went on to tell me that Sharpe had earned about fifty thousand pounds out of the investments Angus made, none of which was recoverable. In the last few weeks Sharpe had also liquidated his original financial investment firm and set up under the new name of Celtic Holdings. It seemed that the liquidation papers for his old firm show more than fifty creditors claiming outstanding debts of about two million pounds. Liquidating the company himself meant that nobody could present a case to the Financial Ombudsman Service. Everything Allan said told me that both he and I were accurate in our descriptions of Sharpe. He finished by saying that he was doing the best he could to try and help Carol and that he would keep in touch either by phone or mail.

'I'm afraid our worst fears are founded,' I said to her after I had finished the call. 'Angus has been completely stitched up by this guy Sharpe.'

'I can't understand why he allowed this to happen,' she responded. 'I mean Angus was a clever and intelligent man.'

'I think sometimes when they get in with a crowd who are completely money orientated these things happen. It's like trying to keep up with the Jones'. Who has got the best car? Who has got the biggest house? Who has got the best looking wife?'

'Well he had all three of those,' Carol responded and let out a coarse sarcastic laugh.

I shook my head in disbelief. 'As Allan said, crazy! There's no other word to describe it.'

We talked some more then she had to see to the children, so I drove back to my bungalow to deal with Bella, make myself a meal, then try and rest. Over the next few days I did drive over to see her during the evening, but the children were always there so we were unable to indulge in any sex. During that time she was receiving regular correspondence from Allan and there was a lot to deal with, which I tried to help her with. She was however a capable young woman and dealt with most of it by herself.

At the weekend I visited the house again to chop some firewood and help out. Afterwards over a cup of coffee we talked some more about the problems. 'What I'd like to do is get to Glasgow to see if I could track down this bloke Sharpe,' I said. (You have to remember that this was the days before internet and computers as we now know them. Nowadays you'd just look it up on the screen and get all the information you needed.) 'Perhaps on Monday you could phone Allan and see if he can find a business address for him. It's bound to be registered somewhere there.' Carol agreed to do that.

I called in again after work on the Monday. Allan had phoned back to her during the day with an address in central Glasgow which one of his lawyer pals there had found. There was also a telephone number.

'What I'd like to do is go there and see if I can confront him,' I said.

'If you do I'm coming with you,' she responded instantly.

'It could get nasty,' I said.

'Good,' she replied. 'I can get nasty too, when I have to.'

I knew there was no point in arguing with her. 'What will you do with the children? We'll be gone all day.'

'They can stay at my friends in Salen for a night. We can spend a night together in a hotel in Glasgow. It's far too long a trip to search around there and come back before the ferry packs up for the night and that way we might get some sex in.' I laughed.

CHAPTER TWENTY

In the following week I took two days off work. I was due some holiday leave anyway. There was nowhere I wanted to go away from the village for a proper holiday so that would be like a little break for me. Carol booked a hotel for us over the phone, near Glasgow city centre, for one night and demanded that she paid for it. I tried to protest but it was no use. 'You're doing this for me,' she berated.

I said to Carol that we ought to check that Sharpe was going to be there on that day, or it would be pointless journey. She agreed to that.

His receptionist answered when I phoned. I used my own name and said I wished to see Sharpe about some investments. She confirmed that he would be in on that day and put my name in his diary.

We set off to catch the first ferry at seven o'clock to the mainland. From the other side of Loche Linnhe it was roughly a two hour journey to Glasgow. Carol drove her Range Rover and she didn't spare the horses. I remember clinging on to the hand strap as we roared through the Pass of Glencoe.

We had to drive around Loch Lomond, which is a magnificent spectacle, with Ben Lomond mountain providing a marvellous backdrop to the water. When we got nearer the city centre there was heavy traffic and motorways which I had become completely unfamiliar with. In a way I was glad Carol was driving as I think she coped with it better as she was used to London traffic. She had booked a room in a Travel Lodge just a mile or so away from the city centre which had parking facilities. We drove straight there and booked in. Once in our room we both jumped on the double bed to test it's springiness.

'This will do for me,' Carol said, while laughing. It certainly did for me as well. It was the most comfortable bed I'd been on in a long time. 'Come on, there's work to do first,' she said. We got up, unpacked our few things into the wardrobes, then on the directions of the reception staff, we caught the bus into the city centre.

Glasgow is a big, bustling busy city. To begin with I couldn't get used to the traffic noise and all the people rushing everywhere. It was a long time since I'd been in such an environment. Carol with her regular trips to London was far more used to such hubbub. From somewhere she had acquired a street map. Over a cup of coffee in a small café we tried to work out the location of Sharpe's office. In a short time we thought we'd sussed it out.

'Before we go there I think I will telephone first,' I said, 'just to make sure he's there at the moment. We don't want to waste our time hanging about.'

We found a phone box and we dialled the number I had dialled before. The same woman receptionist answered and said he was in the office for the morning. I said we would be along soon.

In the required road we found a sign that bore the sign Celtic Holdings on an old nineteen thirties four storey stone building. The sign indicated that the office was situated on the second floor. Carol and I went up a wide stone staircase. Along the passageway a door, on the left hand side, marked Celtic Holdings stood out on semi-glazed frosted glass. I opened it and we went inside.

Sitting behind a typewriter, was a very attractive young woman in perhaps her early thirties, who had jet black shoulder length hair. She was quite stunning.

'I'm Gareth Rees, I phoned earlier,' I said.

'Oh yes,' she replied. 'I'll tell him you're here.' She got up out of her seat and walked towards a closed solid door. Her figure and legs were just as stunning as was the rest of her. She went into the inner room and closed the door behind her. Carol and I were convinced that Sharpe would not know who either of us were when we entered his room. I had never met him before and Carol assured me that she hadn't either. So we hoped to catch him out with the element of surprise.

The glamorous young woman ushered us into the room which was expensively kitted out with upmarket office furniture. Sharpe rose from a high backed leather chair, behind a flash oval desk, to greet us. He was a tall, suave, dark haired man with greying temples. He possessed icy blue eyes and was dressed in a blue shirt, with a white collar over which he wore a dark waistcoat and dark trousers. He came round the desk to shake hands with both of us and I said. 'I am Gareth Rees and this is my friend Carol.' He clearly didn't recognise either of us. 'And I am Edward Sharpe,' he replied and offered us to sit in two leather chairs in front of his desk while he returned to his.

'How can I help?' he said holding out his hand.

I had brought with me a buff coloured file which contained all the details of Angus's investments, which Allan had provided Carol with.

'I understand you advise on investments?' I said.

'I certainly do,' he replied.

'And are you covered by the Financial Ombudsman Service?'

'Indeed,' he said and pointed to a certificate on the wall behind his desk.

'Good,' I responded, then opened up the file and took a sheaf of papers from inside.

'Well, can you tell me how you advised my friend to invest all his money in these schemes which are now almost worthless?' I handed him a sheet of foolscap which contained a list of the investments he had made on Angus's behalf. He looked at the paper and suddenly the look of calm self assurance disappeared from his face. Angus' name was typed on the top of the sheet of paper.

'How did you get hold of this?' he asked while pointing at the paper.

'As I said earlier, Angus was a friend of mine and this is his wife Carol, who is now a widow as Angus committed suicide recently,' I said indicating Carol.

Sharpe's face colour had turned from a slight tan to white in an instant as he read down the list of investments. 'Firstly let me offer Mrs McLeod my sincere condolences, I had no idea that Mr McLeod had died. Especially that way. That must be awful for both of you.'

'Well if you're supposed to be a financial advisor why did you let him invest this amount of money in a scheme that was likely to go bust?' I said.

For a moment he made no reply. Then he put the sheet of paper down on the desk. 'Firstly let me say that this investment scheme had a good track record and had made a lot of money for many of my clients previously. As I'm sure you both know all the financial markets have taken a tremendous nosedive during this last year. Virtually every type of investment dropped dramatically almost overnight. Secondly, I did not know exactly how much money Mr McLeod had in total. Some people like to make out to me that they are very wealthy.'

'But surely as a financial advisor you are required to complete a fact find to ensure that the client has the resources to fund the project.'

'I did indeed, but we can only go on what the client tells us.'

'Is it possible to see a copy of that fact find?' I asked.

'I'm afraid not as it is a company that has now been wound up and it's records destroyed.'

'How convenient,' I replied. 'Why is the Financial Ombudsman unable to pay out Mrs McLeod any compensation? Was your previous firm involved in that organisation?'

'Yes, it was, but only they can tell you why they were not able to pay Mrs McLeod anything. I have no jurisdiction over their actions. They are a government backed body and make their own judgements on each case. You'll have to ask them that.'

'I intend to,' I snapped back.

'Do you want me and my new firm to try and organise some investment schemes to try and make back some of the lost money?' he said.

'Not bloody likely,' I responded. 'Mrs McLeod is virtually destitute. The bank have an order for possession on her home. If they enact that she and the children will be homeless. What have you got to say about that Mr Sharpe?'

'Again I am sorry about that but I had no idea that Mr McLeod was borrowing that sort of money on his home. He never mentioned that to me.'

'Yes, but I bet you encouraged him to invest as much as he could, so you could earn more commission.'

'I didn't do it to earn more commission. I only outlined the growth this fund had made in recent years and the sort of return Mr McLeod might achieve.'

'Pah,' I retorted. 'But that would be on past performance, there is no way you could guarantee that in the future.' I added.

'No, but Mr McLeod did sign a disclaimer which said that he was aware of the risks involved.' Sharpe said.

'So you'd got him sewn up all ways,' I replied.

At that point Carol cut in. Up until then she'd remained silent. 'I've sat here and listened to all this with amazement,' she began. 'Mr Sharpe have you any idea that what you have done has caused me and my very young children horror and extreme distress. As we are unable to claim compensation from anywhere else I think you should refund to me the commission you made on my husband's investments. That at least might get me and my family through the coming weeks financially.' Her voice contained venom.

For a few moments Sharpe was stunned into silence. Again he looked completely startled and bewildered. 'I wish I could do that,' he eventually responded. 'What you have to realise is that we all lost money in the financial crisis, including me. That's why my previous firm went into liquidation. There is no money left from that business. I have had to start here again from scratch to try and make a living. I have to eat and live as well you know. I still think your best bet is to pursue the Financial

Ombudsman. It is their job and purpose to help you with that.'

Carol got out of her chair and stood facing him with her hands defiantly on her hips. 'Well that's what I shall be doing,' she bellowed. 'And I shall be instructing my solicitor to sue you for every penny you've got or haven't got. Come on Gareth, let's get out of here before I become really angry and start throwing things.'

With that she turned on her heels and stormed out of the room. I followed and waved to the brunette as I passed her desk.

To try and calm down we went into a restaurant in the centre of the city for some lunch and to discuss matters further. There, over scampi and chips, we went over the possibilities open to Carol.

'I think we should pursue the Financial Ombudsman people for some compensation. To a certain extent Sharpe was right in saying that it is up to them to pay you out, not him. I mean at the time his previous firm were registered with that organisation, or so he says anyway.'

'I agree with you there,' she replied. 'I also think I should try and sue him personally.'

'Well you ought to contact Allan. He will know how to go about it and if he thinks it's worthwhile. I think you should take his advice on that.'

We agreed and finished with a cup of cappuccino each, something you couldn't get on the peninsula, then we caught the bus back to the Travel Lodge. We hadn't made love for many weeks and we definitely made up for lost time that afternoon and that night.

Then very early in the morning we left the Travel Lodge and set off for the Corran ferry and home.

CHAPTER TWENTY-ONE

In the following week our lives returned to the pattern it had previously adopted. I settled back into my work. Carol tried to pick up the threads of her existence with the children. She made efforts to sell Angus's Mercedes as it would bring in some much needed money and there was no way she needed two cars. A few trips to Fort William were required for that but eventually she found a dealer who was prepared to give her an almost reasonable price. Again it proved that she was quite capable of looking after herself. As before, a couple of days during the week, she called in on me after I had finished work and she had picked up the children from school, armed with some of my badly needed food shopping requirements and an update on her struggles.

During those visits she told me that she had been in touch, by telephone, with the Financial Ombudsman. She added that it was a long and protracted call but at least they agreed to send her a form to complete so they could make an assessment of the situation and come to a decision. She had also been in touch with Allan about suing Sharpe. He had advised caution on that as she could spend a lot of money on going to court and get nowhere. He said he would get back to her once he had made more enquiries with the local Barristers and the like.

At the weekend I went over to her house to help out with chores around the place and chop the firewood. The main requirement for sawing and chopping firewood is to make sure it remains dry otherwise you just get a damp smoky fire which soots up the chimney. I am afraid our sexual liaisons had to be put on a back burner and we could only indulge when the children were away for some time. However, when we did manage to get together it was still very stimulating and enjoyable. All the while though the banks order for possession on the property hung over us like a cloud. Allan had managed to keep them at bay for the time being due to Carol's circumstances but he told her that they would only hold off for so long as the interest on the loan was still mounting. In all that time I never heard from, or saw, Mhairi and neither had Bob or Jessie.

During the following week Carol heard from Allan who advised that after consultations with his legal friends he thought it wasn't worth taking Sharpe to court. His enquiries had led him to discover that Sharpe's current financial business had no registered company accounts and that he probably kept it that way so he could not be sued for any money. At the present Sharpe was also living in rented property so there was no house of his own that you could put a charge on. Both Carol and I and Allan agreed that Sharpe was a clever bastard. She had also received an elongated form from the Financial Ombudsman and I agreed to go over to her house one evening to help her complete it. As usual in the evenings I walked over so as not to draw attention to my visitation.

'I feel like I want to strangle this bloke Sharpe,' she said on my arrival.

'Well if you did that you would end up in jail and where would that leave the kids,' I responded.

'Huh,' she uttered with an impatient sigh.

As she had indicated, the form from the Financial Ombudsman was long and complicated and we continually had delve into Angus' paperwork to discover the answers to their questions. Between us we also wrote a letter to them explaining the situation and Angus's subsequent suicide. Afterwards I played a bit with the children. By then they had got used to me being around the house, and they called me by my first name. When it got near to their bedtime frolic I chased them around the lounge chairs which Carol was grateful for as she said it would get them off to sleep quicker. I left when she took them upstairs to wash and sleep.

On my walk home to my bungalow, despite all the recent trauma, I felt comfortable and happy with my current life and had no regrets about my move north. It was a clear evening, the stars were reflecting on the almost still waters of the stream in front of my gate. Wood smoke was puffing gently out of my bungalow's chimney. Then something above the smoke, in the distance and high in the sky, made me stop and stare. At first I thought it was something to do with my fire, but then I realised it was coming from a long way off and was really miles up. I stood still. It was like an orange glow in the north. I knew it couldn't be lights from a town as there were no towns in that direction, only mountains. As I watched, the colours changed to include reds and greens and blues, yellows, hues I had never seen before. To me it was like a laser light show at an exclusive city disco. Suddenly I realised I was seeing the Northern Lights. What a spectacle. It didn't last long. About five minutes in all, but I stood and watched in awe until it disappeared. I went inside to collect Bella but when we were outside again there was no sign whatsoever of the display in the northern sky, just a million stars remained. The spectacular vision did however fill my dreams that night.

I saw another strange occurrence a few days later. I was driving in Carol's Range Rover to Salen to pick up Cameron, Carol's son, who had been staying with her friend there. The road runs along the shore of Loch Linnhe all the way. There is an attractive boat and yachting harbour in the village. The narrow road itself twists and turns and is tree lined on both sides. At some stages you cannot see the loch for the trees and the bank dropped steeply down to the water. Anyway, halfway there I needed to relieve myself. Rather than embarrass me and Carol's friend by asking if I could use her facilities, I stopped the Range Rover at a convenient pull in, got out and went behind a tree slightly on the down bank so I couldn't be seen from the road, I unzipped my fly and did the necessary. As I was relieving myself I saw the most amazing activity happening at the water's edge, which I wouldn't have been able to see from the road.

Half docked, on a deserted, tiny inaccessible beach was a boat, a bit like a small fishing boat which looked as if it was built for carrying cargo not fish. On the deck I could see small bags or packages about the size of small cement or fertiliser bags. Plodding in the loch, almost up to their waists, were two men carrying the bags and stacking them on the beach. A third man was at the wheel, inside a tiny cockpit, trying to keep the boat steady. I looked about the area and could see no vehicular access to this isolated spot. Where would the packages go from there I thought? And what was in them. Unfortunately I couldn't hang about to find out. I was already a bit late for picking up Cameron and I knew Carol would be getting worried if I was really late getting back with her car and the little boy so I scrambled back up the bank with many thoughts in my mind. From the road I couldn't see anything going on down below there but I had to press on. I said nothing about it to Carol's friend Moira but told Carol about it when I got back to her house.

'Could be smuggling,' she said. 'This coast used to be rife with it years ago. The peninsular survived on it. That's how they lived as they couldn't exist on what they earned and some of them didn't earn anything at all, only what they smuggled,' she said.

That evening I decided to walk down to Jack Banyard's place in the hope I may catch him in. Fortunately he was there and invited me in and I told him what I had seen that afternoon.

'H'm,' he responded. 'Well there's no way you could get a vehicle up or down there.' When I'd told him the exact spot.

'That's what I thought,' I replied.

'I'll have a word with a few people I know who sail regularly up and down the loch to see if they've spotted anything like that or if they know what may be going on. Of course somebody else could be picking the cargo up by boat.' I nodded. 'And I'll inform the coastguard at Fort

William,' he continued. 'They can send a boat up there to try and catch them at it. That's the problem though, catching them at it.'

I gave him the best description I could of the boat. I hadn't spotted any name on the hull. Banyard thanked me for my help. On my way home I called in at the hotel for a pint and spoke to a couple of lads who dabbled with fishing from their small craft and would be active around the loch. None of them had seen anything suspicious like that.

The next day I mentioned the incident to one of my work mates who I knew had a small boat and went out fishing for herring in the loch.

'I've not seen anything like that happening,' Callum replied. 'Tell you what though, I can't do it tonight, but after work tomorrow, if the weather is fine we can take the boat out and you can show me the spot.' I agreed on that and hoped the next day would hold.

Fortunately the following evening was dry and no rain was forecast, although there was a bit of a breeze up. Callum's small craft was kept in his garden and I helped him connect it up to a tow bar on the back of his car. We were able to get the car virtually down to the shore line near the harbour. There was also an outboard motor which I helped affix to the stern. We motored out into the bay and then the wind hit us.

'Cor Blimey!' I shouted when a wave splashed across our bows.

Callum laughed. 'You should be out here when there's a real storm up,' he shouted back.

It took us about twenty minutes to get to the spot where I had seen the events take place. It was certainly a choppy ride. We tried to get in as close as we could to the little bay. 'I don't want to go in too far,' Callum said, 'or we'll get stuck and then we'll have to sit here half the night till the tide comes back up again.'

I pointed to the spot and he slowed the engine to a splutter just to keep us going. He had brought his binoculars with him.

'That certainly is an isolated spot,' he said as he surveyed the scene with the glasses. 'You'd never carry anything big up that bank,' he continued pointing and handed me the bins. 'I mean to get up there by yourself you would virtually have go some of the way up on your hands and knees.' I checked where he was pointing and agreed. 'It must be a two boat job,' he added. 'One crew must dump the stuff here and another boat pick it up. That's what used to happen with the smuggling in the old days. Sometimes the customs would catch them out, but lots of times the smugglers would just get away with it.'

We chugged back to the village harbour braving the strong headwind. Once we secured the boat back onto his car I thought he had earned a drink so we stopped by at the hotel. Like many Scots he downed his pint of beer with a whisky chaser, but while we supped he told me about some of the smuggling stories. He imparted tales of illicit whisky stills in some of the far flung isolated crofts. 'Even nowadays when the families are clearing out their parents old crofts they find bottles of the moonshine in the attic spaces.' We had another round before we left for home.

On the following Monday, in work, Callum told me that he'd been out on his boat fishing on the previous Friday evening by himself. 'I was well over the other side of the water, too far away for me to do anything about it,' he said, 'and it was getting dark, but I could see a boat like you described pulling away from the little beach you showed me. By the time I could have got there nightfall would have completely descended and I would then be putting myself in danger. The other boat was sailing too fast for me get anywhere near it, so all I could do was get myself home. But I thought you would want to know.'

'Thanks for letting me know that Callum,' I said. 'If you'll pardon the pun I think there is definitely something fishy going on there.' He guffawed in his catarrhal Scottish way.

The next time I met up with Carol I mentioned it again to her. 'I think you ought to see Banyard about it again,' she replied.

'Maybe I will,' I responded.

Before doing that however I decided to go and take another look myself. Each time there had been a sighting, either by me or Callum, it had been in the early evening, so one day after work I took Bella briefly around the garden for her visit, then drove in my van down to the Salen road.

This time I parked it away from the previous spot I had stopped in Carol's Range Rover, in a pull-in where I could more easily scramble down the bank to the loch shore. It was still a tortuous slither and I stumbled and slid most of the way, regularly having to grab hold of tree trunks or branches to stop myself from toppling over completely. By the time I reached the bottom I was quite shaken. From where I landed I still couldn't see the little bay as it was over other side of a piece of headland. It therefore required another bout of stumbling over shoreline rocks and boulders to get to the jutting out piece of headland. There I clambered up to the highest point and out of breath I lay down so as not to be seen. As soon as I had gathered my breath I could see the little bay, the tiny beach and also bobbing up and down on the waters edge the same boat, with the same two men plodding through the shallow tide carrying the same size little bags as before and depositing them on the beach. I had brought with me a second hand pair of binoculars I had bought at a pawn shop in Fort William and honed in. It was the same three guys, one holding the wheel on the boat and the two in the water. I stayed and watched for some time, in fact until the two guys had completed the unloading. When they'd done there was a pile on the beach about three foot in height and I guess there were about twenty bags in all. The men clambered back aboard and the boat reversed out of the shallows, swung around and chugged away up the loch, heading inland away from Fort William.

I stayed in my prone position till the boat was out of sight and they couldn't see me, then I clambered down to the beach. Once again it was a perilous trek as I now had seaweed to contend with as well as slippery wet rocks. I nearly went a purler a couple of times. On reaching them I could see the sacks were stacked in three neat piles. They were made of plastic, green in colour with no marking or words on them anywhere.

I bent down and tried to pick one up. It was quite heavy. No way would I have been able to carry that sack back up the bank I had come down. I looked around and concurred that there was no other route back up to the road either. When I pressed on the bag it felt like there was powder inside but they were machine sealed and no way could I pull the tops apart. I looked around for a sharp stone to see if I could smash a small hole in the side. I found something I thought might do it. It took several bashes but I did eventually manage to inflict a tiny pinprick of a hole. I turned the bag on its side and continued hitting it until a tiny file of the powder trickled into my hand. It was white, it had no smell. Of course I had nothing with me to carry it in so I took out my handkerchief, poured it into that, screwed it up tight and tied it at the top in a knot.

By then it was getting dark. I put the handkerchief in my trouser pocket and started up the tortuous scramble back up to my van and my home.

Next day after work I went down to see Banyard at the police station and showed him the contents of my handkerchief. He look at it quizzically then dipped his index finger into the powder, sniffed it then took a tiny lick of it on his tongue. He waited a second to absorb the taste.

'That's heroin,' he said categorically.

'I thought it must be something like that,' I responded.

'You'd better show me where this spot is,' he said.

He drove me down the Salen road in his police car to the spot where I had parked in Carol's Range Rover and we walked to where we could see the little beach. 'There, down there,' I said pointing. 'Last evening when I left there were three stacks of packets of that stuff lying there.' There were none there then.

I explained that there was no way down at that point but I pointed to where I had managed to scramble down.

'There is nothing there now, so I don't see much point in going down,' he said. 'I'll contact the Coastguard and instruct our narcotics boys.' He then drove us back to the police station. 'It's catching them at it, that's the problem,' he continued.

When I got out of his car, he thanked me for my co-operation.

I drove off and called in on Carol. She made me some supper and I told her about my excursion with Banyard. She also told me that Allan was under great pressure from the bank to foreclose on her house. She did however reveal that there might be some relief for her, as the Financial Ombudsman was pursuing their enquiries into Sharpe's affairs. They did indicate that there may be some compensation available but didn't elucidate further.

So, some breathing space for us all. During that week I decided to camp out on the Friday night on the Salen road where I had been before as I had no work to go to on the Saturday morning. I drove my van to the spot where I had parked Carol's Range Rover, then I walked to the rocky peninsular where I had scrambled down before. I'm afraid it was an equally tortuous scramble except this time it was dark which made it even more scary.

Sweating and swearing I reached the rocky outcrop I had previously reached. I slumped down gasping for breath. 'Why am I doing this,' I thought. 'All of this has nothing to do with me.' I lay there for a long time gasping for breath. Darkness was descending rapidly. My binoculars were with me. Through them, in the gloom I could see more packages on the beach. In the distance, in the loch, I could just about make out a small motorised, local type fishing vessel, heading our way from the direction of Fort William.

Whilst trying not to break my neck I slithered once again down the tortuous descent I had previously made to the loch shore. When I reached it, there was still the challenge of the perilous wet loch side rocks to trip and stumble over in the dark before I reached the haven of the short pinnacle I had laid out on before. Once there I crashed out and sweated like a pig. Various deep breaths were required to recover my composure and sense of being. Eventually in the gloom I lifted my binoculars to my eyes and tried to focus in on the decrepit fishing vessel which was heading towards the desolate beach.

I watched closely as it chugged towards the beach. About twenty yards out it stopped and dropped an anchor. Three men on the deck then struggled with a small rowing boat which they dropped into the loch, then got in it themselves and rowed ashore. A few feet off they jumped out and pulled the boat on to the sand. Instantly they began to load the packages from the sand onto the little boat. The whole operation couldn't have taken more than about two or three minutes before they clambered back into the boat and rowed back out to the fishing vessel. I watched as they unloaded the cargo onto the deck, and then themselves. Straining my eyes with the binoculars, as by then it was almost completely dark, I attempted to make out the ships number on the bow of the vessel. It was far too gloomy to read all of it but I could see that the beginning letters were those attached to a Fort William based vessel.

I continued to watch as she chugged away in that direction. Once she was out of sight I got up and scrambled back up the bank I had come down as fast as I my legs would take me. By the time I got to my van I was blowing hard and sweating profusely. However I jumped in and drove like the wind along the narrow twisting road back to the village. There I parked outside the police station. I could see that it was locked and closed up so I drove up to Banyard's bungalow which was about a hundred yards away.

His wife answered the door. 'Is Mr Banyard in?' I asked.

'He is but he's having his meal,' she replied curtly.

'Well can you please tell him that I just spotted a boat with a cargo of heroin on board which I talked to him about the other day.'

She turned her back on me and without saying a word went down the passageway towards the living room. I stood and waited. A few moments later Banyard came to the door still chewing something and wiping his mouth on a serviette.

We both stayed on the doorstep while I explained to him what I had just witnessed. 'Let me put some shoes on and fetch the keys and we'll go down to the station and make some calls.'

I stood for a couple more minutes on the doorstep before he came back chewing on an apple and carrying the office keys. We drove in my van back down to the police station while I elucidated further on what I had seen. He also told me that the narcotics people had confirmed that the powder in my handkerchief was heroin. 'Strong stuff too,' he said. 'They say that lot would be worth a small fortune on the black market.' Inside the office he offered me a seat and moved behind the desk, sat down, then picked up the phone.

'I'll ring coastguard first, see if they can intercept the boat.'

He duly rang the number and related my sightings. Throughout the call I had to continually prompt him on what I had seen including the parts of the boats number I had managed to make out. 'They'll get a boat out there now,' he said when he had finished the call. 'I'd better ring my boys in Fort William as well,' he said. 'See what they can do to help.' He dialled a different number and again throughout the call I had to prompt him on certain of the details.

After he had put the phone down he said, 'That's about as much as we can do from here. You've done well,' he added.

I drove him back to his bungalow and as he got out of the van he said, 'I'll keep you posted on what happens.' He then made for his front door and I drove home to a disgruntled Bella who was distraught at being left on her own all evening.

A couple of days later I had taken Bella for a walk after work when I spotted Banyard's police car pull up in my driveway. I went to the front door to greet him and ushered him in. He took off his police cap as he entered the doorway and I shoved Bella into the kitchen and closed the door, then offered Banyard a seat.

'They managed to intercept the boat,' were his first words. 'Coastguard caught them red handed in the loch outside the Fort. They couldn't outrun their boat. It was full of heroin. The three guys are in the cells in Fort William now talking their heads off. I don't know if they've traced the other three guys in the smaller boat yet but I'm sure they will eventually. I thought you'd want to know.'

'That's great news,' I replied. 'Serves the buggers right. I hope they all get twenty years.'

'I think that's why they're talking their heads off now to try and avoid some of it.'

'Huh', I responded.

'From what we can gather so far the goods would get shipped to Sweden where it has a street value of somewhere in the millions and we guess they get a share of that. I thought you want to know anyway.'

'Sure did, thanks for that,' I responded.

He got up to leave. 'Oh by the way my chief inspector thanks you very much. He wants to meet you personally some time and the Coastguard wants to take you on a loch cruise in their boat. They'll arrange it through me and I'll organise a date when it's convenient to all.' With that he left and I let Bella back into the lounge. She barked and sniffed everywhere in the room where Banyard had been.

'What do you think about all that, girl?' I said. She barked again.

Later in the week an item appeared in the Lochaber news reporting the boarding of the boat by the Coastguard. It went on to say that the men responsible would soon be up before the Procurator Fiscal and committed for trial.

Next day after work I went over to see Carol and told her all that had happened.

'You were very brave. Perhaps they'll give you a medal,' she said.

'I doubt it,' I replied and laughed.

'Anyway I've had some good news as well,' she continued. 'I've had a letter from the Financial Ombudsman saying that it is likely that I may get some compensation because of Sharpe's activities with Angus's money. They say I should be entitled to fifty thousand pounds but it is up to the main board for approval in the coming weeks.'

'That's great news,' I replied.

'It's not going to be hardly enough to pay anything off the bank loan, so I know I am going to have to get out of here sometime soon. Allan tells me that because I am unemployed I should be able to receive some social security money for the children, so we should be able to keep our heads above water for a while anyway.'

'Good,' I responded.

'I ve been thinking about what I should do from here on in,' she continued. 'I don't want to take the children out of school here until at least the end of this school year. What I've thought of is renting a cottage or something like it in the village for the time being. With the money I mentioned we should be able to last out that long. Gareth will you help me look for somewhere.'

'Of course I'll help you. We'll start this weekend.'

'Great,' she replied. 'I'll arrange some viewings and let you know. There's plenty of empty dwellings around the village at this time of year desperate for some income.'

During the Saturday and the Sunday we looked at about half a dozen available rental properties near the village.

Some were awful, some were just about basic, but eventually we both agreed on a traditional highland croft on the loch shore, close enough to walk to the village shop and school. The owner had just died so the family were happy to get an income from the cottage while they sorted out his affairs. The adjacent twelve acres of land were already let out to nearby crofters to graze their sheep on, so there was no problem in that respect. There was the usual hassle about the monthly rental, but eventually we agreed on a compromise between the two amounts. Allan had advised her not to tell anybody about her recompense from the Financial Ombudsman. By then her bank account had been changed into her sole name, so there was no connection between what came into it and Angus' previous dealings.

Through Allan she told the bank that she was prepared to vacate the property, although she would need some time to make arrangements. The bank agreed and gave her twenty eight days notice to quit.

From there on in all hell broke loose. No way could half the furniture and her possessions fit into the newly rented property. She held a garage sale, or the Scottish equivalent of it anyway. I think it was attended by half the population of the peninsular and between the two of us we managed to accumulate a large amount of ready cash.

Then we had to organise a rental van to transport her remaining possessions from one dwelling to the other. It took about a week after my days work to complete all the transportation. At the end of it we were both exhausted. During that time her children stayed with her friend in

Salen, so for most nights we were able to sleep together at her house. It had been some time since we had enjoyed such intimacy but the wait had been worth it.

Then the day came when she had to actually move out. The bailiffs had said that they would arrive at eleven in the morning. The previous night we had slept together. I had taken the following day off work. After breakfast we both walked around every room in the property. She was crying most of the time and I held onto her fervently.

At the appointed hour we could see the bailiff's car coming up the driveway. 'This is it then,' she said.

We went to the front door. The bailiffs approached and she handed them the keys to the property. They took them without saying a word and went inside. I drove Carol in her Range Rover down to her new dwelling at the loch side. Initially it was cold and uninviting but after some time I managed to get the electric night storage heaters to function and a fire going in the grate. We spent the night there listening to the waves on the loch shore through the open bedroom window.

After those hectic few weeks life settled back into some form of normality. Carol's children joined her at the new dwelling and thoroughly enjoyed playing on the loch shore, 'I told you kids of that age would settle anywhere. They're very adaptable,' I repeated.

'Of course you did. You're always right,' she replied sarcastically.

Then a few days later I received a visit from Banyard who gave me a couple of dates to go to Fort William to meet up with the Police Inspector and the coastguard. I arranged to take a day off work on one of the dates and they agreed that Carol could go with me. We had a wonderful time. The Police Inspector welcomed me warmly and in fact presented me with a certificate for my co-operation with the force.

'There you are I told you they'd give you a medal,' Carol said on our way out of the police station. I laughed.

In the afternoon we had a marvellous boat trip with the coastguard on their vessel. Fortunately, for once up there, the weather was good and they took us to many of the unexplored coves on the loch. Fabulous views.

In the evening we drove home to Strontian a very happy and contented couple.

CHAPTER TWENTY-TWO

Developments with Carol's fifty thousand pounds compensation from the Financial Ombudsman soon occurred after that. She had to sign an agreement which she took to her solicitor Allan to see. 'I don't think you will get a much better offer than that,' he said after he had read the form. She signed it in front of him and he agreed to post it on to them with a covering letter reaffirming her widowed status and Angus's recent suicide in the hope they might hurry the payment up. Within a short time the money was in her bank account and by then she was also receiving social security payments for her children, so for the time being anyway, she was financially solvent.

For a period of time matters concerning us appeared to go relatively smoothly. In my work we were starting on a new fence line which we had to sail across an inland loch to reach. It was another very awe inspiring boat trip, both ways. The views up there were also spectacular, although it made it a longer day and I was quite bushed when I got home. Carol would sometimes call in with the kids when I got home and she continued to do some of my shopping for me. At weekends we would quite often embark on trips around the peninsular in her Range Rover, with Cameron and Rachel on the back seats. Since I'd been living there I had never really had the opportunity to do that as I really hadn't trusted my little van to get up some of steep, narrow, twisting roads, whereas the Range Rover was ideal for the job. There were some wonderful little isolated bays and coves which I could only marvel over.

When we could, which wasn't often, we would still cohabit and I remained enthralled by her body and looks.

Gradually however, I spotted a change come over her. She was generally fine with me, but I noticed she was getting ratty with the children, something she had never been before. I wondered if it was some form of delayed shock after Angus's suicide. I tried to talk to her about it but she brushed my words off by saying it was just tiredness. She said living in the cottage alone with just the children, at their age, was hard going, as before Angus had always been around most of the time and he applied most of the discipline.

Then when we had a meal together I noticed she drank more wine than before. Previously if the children were about she would only drink, say half a glass of white, but by then she was polishing off two full glasses in big gulps. Then one evening I caught her out. I'd gone down to see her after dark. By then I had a key to the cottage. I always knocked loudly on the door first then let myself in with the key. I'd caught her out though. She was slumped over the dining room table with her head in her hands and crying. In front of her, on the table, was one empty bottle of white wine and one half empty one. She looked up at me in horror.

'What's going on?' I said.

'Oh Gareth, I didn't want you to see me like this,' she replied and got up out the chair and fell into my arms. 'I just don't know what I am going to do.'

'Tell me about it,' I said.

'It's too embarrassing.'

'I'm here to help. You haven't got anybody else near at hand to tell,' I remonstrated.

'Oh Gareth,' she said while she was still in my arms. I was kissing her tear stained face. 'I've been so worried and afraid to tell anybody, especially you.'

'Tell me what. What's the problem?' There were more tears.

'I've got a lump on my breast.' She touched her right breast as she said it. 'I've been to see the doctor and he is sending me to Oban for tests.'

'Oh gosh. How long have you known about it?'

'About two weeks now.'

'What am I going to do with the children if I have to go into hospital for a stay?' She was still clinging on to me and sobbing.

'Well we'll cross that bridge when we come to it. Have you a date for tests yet?'

'No, the doc says they will write to me, but you know what they're like, it'll probably be weeks away.'

I stayed with her for another hour or so till she stopped sobbing. I said, 'It's quite a common operation nowadays for woman. It usually turns out fine. If it goes OK it tends to be more of a psychological problem afterwards than a physical one. My aunt had both her breasts removed and she was much older than you. She was in her sixties and if I remember correctly she lived to her eighties.'

I offered to stay with her but she didn't want that with the children in the cottage. 'I could sleep on the sofa,' I said.

'No I'd be tempted to come and get you,' she replied.

I laughed. We hugged and kissed some more and I left with a promise to call in to see her after work next day.

'I'll cook you a meal,' she said as I went out through the door. I blew her a kiss as I got into my van. She smiled back at me.

The next few days with her were difficult. It was still obvious that she was having a problem controlling her emotions. She was such a beautiful woman and I guess it would have been catastrophic for her to lose even one of her breasts, let alone two. We both waited daily for the appointment letter to come from the hospital, but as it is with these things they take their own time to deal with it, which to the sick and unwell is an interminable wait.

During those days I could tell she wasn't happy but I did my best to try and cheer her up. Sex was an indulgence which gradually she didn't want to partake in. I perfectly understood how she felt about that. The appointment date at the hospital eventually materialised and on the day I took a holiday day off work and drove her there in the Range Rover.

The staff there were curt but efficient and they told us that they would be in contact with Carol's doctor in the village. We drove home wondering how long that would take.

After a week or so it took various telephone calls to Doctor Masson to procure the results of the tests. He said she should come in to see him at his daily clinic.

As with everything in the highlands patience is required. To avoid the queue at the surgery, one morning Carol and I went there at about nine o'clock in the morning. Nobody else was around.

When we arrived Doctor Masson came out from his room. 'Oh hello you two. I'm afraid you're going to have to excuse me for five minutes.' To me he looked exhausted. 'I'm afraid I've been out all night and I need a coffee and some breakfast.'

We agreed to that and he was gone some ten minutes into the school canteen next door and then returned to say, 'Thank you, I needed that.'

At the time Doctor Masson was the only doctor on the Ardnamurchan peninsular. He had a territory of three hundred square miles to cover by himself. He also had a heart condition that eventually killed him. Many times during the week he had to get himself out of bed at one o'clock in the morning to go up half a mountain in snow and minus temperature degrees to deal with old people clinging on to survive in an ancient croft, which would have had no running water or electricity. By today's standards of medicine he was a hero. When he wanted a holiday he had to move out of his Salen bolthole, with his precious boat and beautiful loch side garden, to provide accommodation for the two weeks he was off work to the locum who had to step in for him during that period. His only recourse, to placate his wife, was to take her on a continental cruise. He once admitted to me that he hated that like hell.

He sat us both in chairs alongside his desk. He picked up a file which obviously contained details of Carol's scan. 'I'm afraid it not good news,' he said after glancing at the file.' I noticed Carol's head hang down. 'There is definitely a lump which is cancerous and needs removing. It will require an operation I'm afraid.'

'Oh dear,' Carol responded.

'The operation will not be a big one. With any luck you'll only need to stay in one night.' Carol and I looked at each other but said nothing.

'Would you like me to arrange it with the hospital?' he asked then continued. 'I think you should do it quickly as the lump could grow and cause more trouble. The operation should prove definitely if it is cancerous or not.' He looked straight at her waiting for an answer.

She looked across at me and said, 'What do you think Gareth?'

I replied, 'I think it's best to get it over and done with quickly. A small operation, which might only require one nights stay isn't going to be the end of the world and it's all for your benefit anyway.' I could see Doctor Masson nodding his head in agreement.

'I think as Gareth has said, I'll have it done and get it over with please.' Carol said to the Doctor.

'Good,' he replied. 'I'll organise it, but you'll get the letter from the hospital. They'll probably want to see you beforehand to talk about the operation and take some tests, but that's nothing to worry about at all. It will probably only take an hour.'

We both thanked him, shook hands and left.

'Oh dear,' Carol said when we were outside.

'Whatever, you're doing the best thing,' I replied.

This time the response from the hospital was more rapid. As the appointment was for a weekday and she was only going to be there for an hour or so she decided to go alone. We agreed that it would be silly for me to take more time off work when I would be more needed at the operation time. I remember it was a Wednesday afternoon when she set off for Oban by herself.

After work and taking Bella out for her walk I drove down to the cottage. 'How did it go?' I asked when I was inside.

'Oh that was quite easy,' she replied. 'It was mainly blood tests, plus a cardiogram, and blood pressure and pulse tests.' She sounded quite upbeat. 'But they asked me enough questions to fill a book. They have my life history

I think. They say I should hear about a date for the op in a day or two.'

'Good,' I responded. 'Best to get it over with quickly.'

'I agree,' she said.

Afterwards she made me a meal and we sat down at the dining room table to eat it with Cameron and Rachel. They were both quite used to my company by then and we were almost like a family unit. When we finished eating they went out to play in the garden, I asked Carol, 'What are you going to do with them when you go into hospital?'

'My friend in Salen has agreed to have them for a few days,' she said. 'I don't know what I would do without her, or you, for that matter.'

'That's what friends are for,' I replied with a chuckle.

We washed up and then went down to join the kids at the loch side.

'There you are,' I said pointing at the children frolicking at the edge of the water. 'I told you that kids of that age would settle anywhere.'

'Of course you did. You're always right,' she said sarcastically.

I laughed and twiggled my thumb on my nose at her.

*****

Around about that time I noticed some of the village people's attitude to me change, particularly amongst the old folk and more particularly the older women. You have to understand that most of the older folk on the peninsular belonged to Free Church of Scotland, or the 'wee frees' as they were known. The members of that tradition have very strict rules on morals. They don't drink, they don't smoke and they only eat specific foods on certain days. On Sunday they don't go out except to Church, to which they go three times during that day. For the rest of the day they stay indoors reading The Bible. On the Sabbath they are not allowed to do any gardening or to hang out washing or use a lawn mower or any kind of machinery, and those who did would entail a penance and were frowned upon.

As I have mentioned before gossip about anybody and everybody soon gets around the village like a wild fire. I guess in my case, the word about me and Carol cohabiting, for want of a more apt description had circulated widely. The 'wee frees' would think of that as being morally corrupt. Sex was only allowed in the sanctity of marriage and mainly for the purposes of raising children. So in time I noticed that the older women began to ignore me. Those who had acknowledged me before with a cursory glance began to look the other way when I passed them even if I said 'hello.' The men were much the same, although if I said 'hello' to them they would usually just nod their head or grunt in response.

I mentioned this to Carol. 'Oh, the old locals have always been like that,' she replied. 'When I first came here the 'wee frees' used to cold shoulder me because I sometimes wore a mini skirt or in the summer a skimpy top. I should just ignore them. Anyway their numbers are dwindling. Only a handful of them are left. The church is now half empty on a Sunday, whereas when I first came here it was full every week.

Afterwards I recalled my work mate Tommy telling me that one Saturday lunch time he was walking down the road to the hotel, to imbibe his usual weekly intake of beer and whisky chasers. That day it happened to be lashing down with rain and he was getting soaked. When he was half way there one of the wee frees stopped by his side in his car. The driver rolled down the side window and said, 'I'll take you down to the village, but I'll not drop you at the hotel.' Tommy readily agreed as he was getting soaked, but he had to walk from the village square to the hotel and continued to get soaked for the rest of the way.

CHAPTER TWENTY-THREE

A few days later a date for Carol's operation arrived in the post. It would take place on a day early in the following week. As the time grew closer I noticed her get edgy again, but I could hardly blame her for it was going to be a traumatic event for a young woman with her looks and figure.

The evening before I drove her and the two children in the Range Rover to her friends house in Salen where the children were going to stay. There were tearful farewells. She had told the kids that she was going into hospital for an operation but had not told them what it was for. On the way back she was upset and sobbed.

'Come on,' I said, 'they have told you that you may only be in for a couple of days and you won't know anything about it when they operate on you. And when it's all over you'll be mended.'

'I know, it's just what they have to do with me afterwards that worries me. I may have to have chemotherapy. That would be awful.'

'Well we'll cross that bridge when we come to it,' I replied. For the rest of the journey home I had to continually console her.

Next day I took a day off work and drove her to the hospital. The nurse who received us was very kind and helpful. 'As you've come from over the water I don't think it's worth you coming back again tonight as she will be more or less knocked out and asleep,' the nurse said to me. 'I'll give you the ward's phone number and it's best if you phone in the morning to see how she has got on.'

I agreed to that. Carol and I hugged and kissed and then I left and let them get on with what they had to do.

I drove home, via the ferry, with a heavy heart and worried mind. To try and clear my head I took Bella out for a decent late night walk. When I got to bed though I had difficulty in sleeping and tossed and turned all night.

I had kept the Range Rover in my drive so next morning before seven o'clock I drove down to the cottage to use Carol's phone and dialled the hospital. After I got through to the ward they told me that the operation had gone well and that she had been asleep most of the time since. I asked if it was worth me coming over after work. The nurse said, 'It should be, as we hope to have her out of here in a day or two. Perhaps you had better phone first though.'

I still fretted most of the day. After work I drove to the hotel in the Range Rover and phoned the hospital from there. They said it was OK for me to come over for visiting that evening. I grabbed a toasted sandwich in the hotel bar and drove across to Oban wondering what I might find there.

I was surprised to be greeted by a smile. Carol was sitting up in bed. I bent over and kissed her. She couldn't do much with her arms as they were attached to drips and feeds. She was still wearing a surgical overall. I sat on the bedside chair. I'd brought with me some grapes and a magazine.

'Well you don't look too bad,' I said. 'How do you feel?'

'Doped up,' She replied. 'They've obviously got me on some drip painkiller or tranquilliser as I keep falling off to sleep. I'll try not to do that while you're here, but if I do you'll have to forgive me.'

'Just to see your pretty face is enough for me.' That brought another smile. 'Did it all go OK?' I asked.

'Well as you know I knew nothing about the op, but they say it all went well and that they got everything.'

'When will they let you out?' I asked.

'They say in couple of days if things continue to progress well, but I'll have to come back soon afterwards for some tests.'

We left it at that with me agreeing to go over on the ferry to take her home on whatever day, after I had finished work. On my way out of the ward I spoke to the nurse who I had met before.

'Is she OK?' I asked.

'Yes,' she replied. 'but she's going to need some care when she gets home.'

I made the long journey back across the ferry and through the glen still pondering. I didn't go back again for a couple of days but I used her phone to call the hospital on each one. They said she was progressing. Then one day they said that she would be ready to go home on the next day. I said I would pick her up after work. They agreed to that.

On my way there I picked up some of the clothes that she'd asked for from the cottage, then drove in the Range Rover over the ferry, eating a sandwich for my tea as we sailed.

Carol was sitting up in a chair when I arrived and looked quite perky, and she was dressed. I was treated to another good smile and we enjoyed a prolonged kiss, interrupted by the nurse. 'That's enough of that,' she said. 'There will be plenty of time for that when you get home. I've got to get her organised to leave now.'

I handed Carol the clothes I had brought with me. 'Thank heaven for that,' she said. 'I'll change now as I'm sure these ones I've got on will stick to me before long.'

The nurse shooed me away and drew the blinds around the bed. I had to cool my heels in the passageway from where I could hear the nurse giving her a list of instructions and tablets and saying that they had organised the district nurse to visit her at the cottage next day.

The drive home was fairly sedate. I didn't want to rock her around too much after all she'd been through. Fortunately when we were on the water it was fairly calm and she coped well. We decided that as the children were still at her friends house in Salen we would spend the night together. Between us we produced a meal. Afterwards I went to fetch Bella to join us and she slept in the kitchen of the cottage. In bed there was no attempt by either of us to indulge in sex. We both crashed out as soon as the light was out.

Early the next morning we were both up at about six o'clock. She seemed to be reasonably perky although a bit shaky. She made me some breakfast, then drove me and Bella to my bungalow to await the forestry Land Rover at seven thirty, for my days work. We again exchanged a passionate kiss. That day I found the work to be a tiring exercise, but I have to confess that I found some consolation in the fresh mountain air and the combative company of my work pals. By then they knew all about my relationship with Carol and her troubles and it was just what I needed to drag me out of my despair.

Again after work I picked up Bella and headed for the cottage. Carol was a bit depressed. She confessed she was aching all over. The District Nurse had been that morning and helped her with the tablets, what to take and when. In amongst them were painkillers which she had to take three times a day, she said, they made her feel drowsy. The nurse had promised to call back next morning. From what I could gather it was the same nurse who visited me in my time of trouble. While I took Bella for a walk along the loch side Carol cooked a meal for both of us. Afterwards I suggested that I again stay the night to keep her company, but she refused the offer.

'I've got to get used to coping by myself,' she added. 'And the children are coming home tomorrow.'

Her friend at Salen, Louise, was going to pick up Cameron and Rachel from school and bring them to the cottage afterwards. We agreed that I wouldn't go to visit that evening so as to let them all get used to each other again.

'If I'm desperate and panic stricken I can drive them and me up to your place and scream my head off,' Carol pronounced.

We agreed to that but I said, 'If you're going to scream your head off you'd better go and do it over the other side of the mountain and I'll keep watch over children in the bungalow.' We both laughed.

It was the following evening after work when I visited the cottage again. We all shared a meal together and afterwards we went down the loch side to play with the kids. Carol admitted that this was the best way of getting them to go to sleep when they went to bed. I could see that although she was putting on a brave face for them, underneath the pretence she was still very strained and uncomfortable.

'I do sleep a lot during the day,' she volunteered. 'But I have to remember to put the alarm on or else I'd sleep right through to the night.'

At that time Louise was still picking up the kids from school and dropping them off at the cottage on her way home to Salen with her own children. Carol told me that she had communication from the hospital. They wanted to see her again to discuss everything in the following week. I offered to drive her there but she would have none of it as it would mean me having to take another day off work. 'I have to get myself moving again properly,' she said. 'I'm going to start picking up the kids from school this week, so that will get me driving again.' I reluctantly agreed as there wasn't anything externally physically wrong with her at that time and she also needed to see other people rather than just me.

At the weekend the four us had another trip out in the Range Rover to the remote outposts on the peninsular, I usually drove. Seeing some of these places for the first time was another eye-opener on how life in the remote corners of the highlands was and had been. Most of the smaller, older cottages were still without running water and electricity. In comparison even to the laid back state of our village they were like going back to another century. They were mostly occupied by older folk. Some of the women still wore headscarves all day and the men hats of various description. A lot of the land was stripped bare because of the relentless onshore gales from the Atlantic, but there were the occasional crofts occupied by younger families. Crops were out of the question because of the wind. The crofters usually had sheep, some cattle, pigs and chickens and could just about manage a cut of hay in the summer to feed them through the winter. Fuel for their fires was provided by peat which involved digging the peat on their land in the summer for that purpose. Most of their electricity was provided from petrol driven generators on their site.

Carol's appointment at Oban hospital during the following week occurred without my intervention. After work that day Bella and I travelled in my van to the cottage to see she how she had got on. By then she'd picked the children up from school and sounded quite upbeat when I arrived.

'How did it go?' I asked after we had embraced. By then Cameron and Rachel were used to our minor indulgences in semi passion.

'Here they go again,' Cameron once remarked to our embarrassment when we were indulging.

'OK, I suppose,' she replied. 'They want to see me in another month.' You have to remember that these were the days before radiology treatment after breast removal. 'I told them that the implant nearly drove me mad, but they said I would get used to that and for the next month the district nurse would come to see me once a week and I was to tell her if there were any problems.'

So there we are, that's how it was left and Carol, I and the children were left to manage by ourselves as best we could. That night we all shared a meal and Carol and I indulged in a glass of wine.

As the days went on I could see she was still struggling mentally and physically to cope, but she mostly presented a brave face and I did my best to occupy the children when I was at the cottage. It did worry me though. Monetary wise, at that time, she was just about able to cope but I worried about what she was going to do when the six month tenancy on the cottage was up. The summer season was approaching and the owners would want to either put the rent up substantially or let it to the summer visitors.

By then the bank had foreclosed on the London flat so that was another outlet that was no longer in existence for her and the children.

'Where are you going to go from here?' I said to her one evening as we were sitting by the loch side watching the children play.

'I just don't know Gareth. I've racked my brains and I'm just about at my wits end about what to do.'

CHAPTER TWENTY-FOUR

At that time our lives had more or less returned to some sort of normality. She occasionally got ratty with either me or the children, but I suppose it was to be expected after what she had been through, so the three of us let it pass. The children occasionally raised their eyebrows in my direction when she was having one of her 'paddies' and we just got on with what we were doing, although Rachel did sometimes answer her back.

By then we were almost like a normal family unit although we didn't live together. When the children were not around, which wasn't often, we did manage to partake in some sex. In that respect the implant made little difference. As far as I was concerned she was still a very beautiful woman.

Before her six month tenancy in the cottage was up we started to look around for alternative accommodation for her and the children. The owners of the cottage had told her that they would have to put the rent up to summer prices as that was the only way they could cover their costs over the year. That price was far more than Carol could afford. She couldn't go too far from the village because of getting the children to the village primary school, which was within walking distance of the cottage if they really wanted some exercise or didn't have the car.

Frankly most of the properties we saw during our search were nowhere near the standard of where she was currently living. At a price she could afford many of them were run down and in need of decoration and more up to date kitchen and bathroom facilities. Some were ex-council house, terraced properties in the centre of the village, with no suitable areas for the children to play in or proper parking, except for on the road outside.

The days ticked by and the expiry date of the tenancy got nearer. 'Gareth I'm beginning to get worried. I'm going to be homeless soon,' she said to me one day.

Each time we met we talked over the possibilities endlessly but we could not really come up with any sensible alternatives. We continued to look at other houses and cottages but none of them, at a price she could afford, were suitable. We concluded that she had been very lucky to find the one she was currently in.

Then, out of the blue one evening, I said almost as a joke, 'Well you'll just have to come and live with me then.'

Her response utterly surprised me. For many moments her blue eyes stared at me and she said nothing. Then her face exploded into a smile. 'Oh Gareth do you think that's possible? You'd have to cope with me, and the children.'

I guffawed. 'I think I could just about stand it' I replied jokingly. 'Anyway we half live together at the moment. All villagers now know of our relationship and those that don't like it can go and stuff themselves.'

She laughed.

'There's plenty of room at my place. I've got three bedrooms, two of which I never use except for storage.

There's a big garden for the kids to play in and a stream out front as well. It's not quite the manor house you were used to living in and if it all gets too much for me I can drown the little buggers down there.'

'Oh Gareth don't even think of such a thing. The manor house was great, but you should have seen some of places I used to live in when I was struggling in London before I met Angus.'

'I was only joking.' I added. 'We all seem to get on quite well together.'

'Yes,' she replied. 'They do like you.'

We talked some more about the idea. 'You would be surrounded by all their toys,' she said.

'Well we'll have to teach them to be tidier. Bella won't stand for a mess. She'll tell them.'

'OK, You'd better leave it with me. I'll have to break the news gently to them to get their true response.'

So I let her get on with what she proposed to do which was to sell me as a person and my bungalow to Cameron and Rachel. They had of course been to my bungalow in the daytime many times recently when we were all going out somewhere. When we got together at the weekend Carol said to me, 'I think I have managed to persuade them into the idea. Anyway, we are going to have to do something pretty quickly as my tenancy here runs out in a few weeks.'

'Tell you what,' I said, 'why don't you bring them over tomorrow and I can show them properly around the place and the garden. We can go out for a picnic and then go back to the bungalow afterwards for a meal. That way they can get used to the feel of the place.'

'What a good idea,' she replied with a smile. 'I'll cook the meal if you like. I guess I'll have to get used to your stove if it's all going to work out.'

'Oh good,' I chuckled. 'You can't have two cooks in the kitchen. Does that mean you'll cook my breakfasts as well when you move in?'

'We'll see about that,' she quickly responded. So that's what we organised for the next day, which was a Sunday.

Mid morning the three of them turned up in the Range Rover. Firstly I showed them around the garden. Fortunately it was a sunny day. The children roamed around the open space happily. We discussed that there was enough room for them to ride around it on their bikes without having to go out on the road. Inside they looked around all the rooms. Carol and I let them go by themselves although Bella followed them everywhere. By then she was used to them and they with her. Cameron came out of one of the bedrooms and said, 'There are bunk beds in here. Can I have the top one?'

'We'll see in due course,' Carol replied.

Then I took them all down to the stream. That was the pièce de résistance. The two kids frolicked on the little beach alongside it. Carol had to stop them from going into the water to paddle. Bella barked and chased them as they cavorted about.

'This is great,' Cameron said. 'Can I have a fishing rod please?'

Carol for about the sixth time said, 'We'll see in due course,' and looked sceptically at me.

Before they were dirty and wet we went back to the bungalow and the Range Rover to embark on our picnic, which Carol had prepared. Again we continued with our exploration of the more distant parts of the peninsular including the famous Ardnamurchan lighthouse, which is the most westerly lighthouse in Great Britain and faces all the elements straight off the Atlantic. We had our picnic on the shores of a small inland lochan. Afterwards we continued our tour, before driving back to the bungalow. It had been a happy day. Carol and I just hoped the peace would last.

At my home the two children played in the garden with strict instructions not to go to the stream. I shut and bolted the gate to ensure they didn't, then went in to help Carol with the meal. There was the usual kerfuffle about where the pots, pans and utensils were, but we managed reasonably well without having a proper argument. I was then to fetch the kids in while she dished up the meal. I was given further instructions to supervise them washing their hands. I could see that this was going to be a complete change in lifestyle for me. I did hope I would be able to cope with it. Bella watched it all with fascinated interest.

We enjoyed the meal and laughed and joked a lot. They were really good company. I, of course had never experienced anything like it in my life before.

Then they got into the Rover for the journey home. Carol and I hugged and kissed before she got in. 'We've had a wonderful day. Thank you,' she said.

'A pleasure,' I replied and kissed her again. When she was inside she looked at me and showed me her crossed fingers, then smiled. I watched them drive off and waved. The children waved back. During the next week I told my landlords of my plans which they were happy with and we negotiated a new one year lease, although they did put the rent up. Over the next week or so, bit by bit, we moved her possessions out of the cottage and into my bungalow.

To save money this time we used my van. The children helped or usually got in the way and Bella was almost as much of a nuisance. She had to sniff every item we brought in and constantly got under our feet causing us to nearly trip over her repeatedly. I had to bite my tongue, as the children were around, to stop myself from swearing at her.

Over the final weekend before her tenancy expired we moved the final bits and pieces of her possessions and their clothes. On the Sunday afternoon they made the move complete. Beforehand Carol and I had decided that we wouldn't sleep together at this stage. Carol would sleep in the second bedroom which was almost as big as mine and the two kids initially would share the third and sleep in the two bunks.

Almost immediately there was an argument between the two of them as to who was going to have the top bunk. Carol had to intervene quickly. It was the first time I had really heard her let loose at them in that manner. I kept well out of the way. Eventually a compromise was reached that they would take it in turns, on a weekly basis to occupy the top one. I could see straightaway that this was all going to be 'fun.' Somehow or another we got through that first night. When I got up next morning at six thirty for work Carol was up to make my breakfast. What a treat!

CHAPTER TWENTY-FIVE

And so my solitary life of peace and tranquillity was turned overnight into a permanent riot. Fortunately, as I had to start work at seven thirty in the morning I was up and able to use the bathroom before the two children were about. Carol continued to make my breakfast, so I was able to have a peaceful half hour with her to talk over the matters of the day while I ate, before going out to meet the Forestry Land Rover. In work I had to take a lot of good humoured stick from my workmates about my newly acquired family. It was only when the children went out to an after school event in the village that we were able to indulge in some sex.

With the benefit of hindsight I could say I gradually got used to it all and in a way began to enjoy it. For the first time in my I life I had something to occupy my mind other than work or my own personal problems. And I guess I began to enjoy being a pseudo Dad. After the first week or so I actually bought Cameron a fishing rod and together we began to learn how to fish in the stream. We didn't catch much but we had some good times together. To compensate Carol bought Rachel a new bike. Gradually the people we knew and liked in the village called around to see us to wish us luck. Thankfully Bob and Jessie approved after I had taken Carol and the kids to meet them. They confirmed that they had still not seen or heard anything about Mhairi which continued to worry me. Unfortunately I was too busy at the weekends to go clambering up to her cave to try and see her. Bella had also become very stoic and gradually began to quietly suffer the children's shenanigans.

So we fell into a routine and became what you may call a normal family unit. By then most of the village began to accept us as such except for the hardened Wee Frees. We even started to attend some of the village social events and I enjoyed most of them, something I had never embarked on when on my own.

Carol and I also began to talk about our own personal situation. Cohabiting like that wasn't something either of us were really happy with. We both agreed that if we were going to go on living together that we should seek a more permanent arrangement.

'OK, will you marry me please?' I blurted out quickly and mockingly went down on one knee.

'Are you being serious?' she responded.

'Of course I am,' I replied remaining on one knee. 'Where am I going to find anybody nicer and more beautiful than you.'

For a second she didn't reply. I thought she was going to refuse then she said, 'I couldn't think of anything more I could possibly want. Yes please.' So I got off my knee and we hugged and kissed.

We discussed that it was coming up to a year since Angus's death and we would hold off the wedding until after that anniversary and that we wouldn't tell the children until that date had passed.

We did however organise a trip to Fort William on a Saturday to purchase an engagement ring. We didn't tell the kids the purpose of our journey. They went to their school friends at Salen for the afternoon. Carol and I had fun in town and a few animated discussions before we settled on a ring which suited both of us. It was white gold with a diamond stone in the centre. When we picked the children up we still didn't tell them of our plan as it was still a few weeks to go until the anniversary of Angus's death and Carol didn't wear the ring until after that date. While we'd been in the Fort she had also bought a few clothes and bits and pieces for the children which covered up the purpose of our visit. And so, for a short while, life went on as before.

On the actual anniversary of Angus's death we all went down to his grave in the cemetery to pay our respects. The four of us all bought flowers to adorn his small tombstone. I think Carol was actually the most upset of us all and she did snivel and cry a bit, which affected the children, so we did not tell them of our plans till a week or so afterwards.

When we did so it was one evening after our evening meal while we were all still sitting around the dining table. As kids tend to do they both took it all in good spirits, almost unconcerned, as though it was something that was inevitable anyway. After we'd talked Carol went to fetch her engagement ring to show them. Again they both seemed pretty unimpressed. She wore the ring from that day onwards.

When they had gone out into the garden afterwards I said to Carol, 'There you are, I told you that kids of that age are adaptable.'

'Of course you're always right,' she responded mockingly.

We decided to make the wedding a quiet affair. As neither of us had attended at the local church except for Angus's funeral we thought we would opt for a registry office ceremony in Fort William. We managed to persuade Tony and Kay, two new friends we had made in the village, to accompany us and act as witnesses. They both came up to the highlands for their retirement after spending all their lives in North Wales, so I had quite a bit in common with them and they were good fun. Carol had to make a few trips to Fort William to make the necessary arrangements. Between us we had very little money to fall back on so we only organised a small buffet reception at the hotel in the village afterwards. We intended to invite a few other friends we had made in the village along with a couple of my more civilised work pals and their wives. In all though, besides us, there would be no more than a dozen guests, but I did order some champagne. The days leading up to the date were busy. Carol decided against a wedding dress and bought a small neat two piece suit and I managed to resurrect my one remaining old work suit to wear, although she did take it to the dry cleaners in Fort William beforehand on one of her many visits there. The day eventually came round and the six of us all travelled to Fort William one Saturday in the Range Rover for our late morning appointment. Carol and I had decided that from that night onwards we would sleep together in my bedroom. We had told the children before but all they did was kick up a ruckus about who would sleep in the bedroom Carol had been occupying. Again we agreed on a compromise that for the time being they would use it in turn, on weekly basis, as they had done before with the top bunk. Life was never going to be easy or simple again I thought.

It was a happy Saturday and we all had a good laugh. Tony acted as best man and passed over the wedding ring I had bought and afterwards we joked all the way home in the Range Rover. The children were very good. The reception in the Hotel was a bit of a riot and we all drank too much champagne.

That night Carol and I went to bed together for the first time as a married couple and it was marvellous.

CHAPTER TWENTY-SIX

And so life went on much as it had been before. The children had good days and bad when they argued with each other incessantly. When they were home Carol spent most of the time acting as a referee between them. I was glad I went out to work early in the morning before they were up or I don't think I could have coped. Carol was usually pleased to see me arrive home at four o'clock.

The days however sped by. Carol had no real repercussions from her mastectomy. We spent more time with the friends we had made in the village, which was good fun and by then we were accepted round and about as a normal established married couple. Cameron continued to fish in the stream. He became quite good at it and actually caught some fish. Rachel was making more friends at school and would occasionally bring them home to play, which ensured more chaos prevailed.

Then very early one morning all hell broke loose. I was awoken some time before six o'clock by what appeared to be a banging noise on the back door and Bella began barking. I struggled out of bed in my shorts. In doing so I had woken Carol up. 'What's that?' she called out.

'I don't know I'm going to find out.'

When I entered the kitchen Bella was sniffing at the back door.

'What is it old girl,' I said and went to open it. On the back step I couldn't believe what my eyes saw. Bella leapt outside and started sniffing it. 'Oh bloody hell,' I said to myself as I bent down to pick it up. Straight away I knew what it was.

Wrapped in a blanket lay a baby. The name Eilidh was scrawled on a tiny piece of paper attached to the blanket by a pin. I bent down to pick the child up and walked out into the back garden to look for anybody who might be around, but of course there was nobody. When I re-entered the bungalow Carol was up and standing in the kitchen wearing her dressing gown.

'What on earth's that?' she said.

'It's a baby,' I responded.

'I can see it's a baby, but what's it doing here?' Bella continued to sniff around me and the child.

'It's a long story. I'll try and explain later. We'd better check her over first. See if she's OK. Will you help? I'm not much good at this sort of thing.' We quickly concluded that it was a baby girl.

Carol moved towards me and took the child out of my arms and said, 'She's very pretty,' and began to remove the blanket. We moved into our bedroom and began to inspect her on the bed. 'You've obviously got some explaining to do,' she added as we began to check the child. 'You'd better get some milk and a bath towel. Let's see if she will take some milk.' I moved quickly to fetch both items. She accepted the milk although she cried and sniffled a bit. After a while Carol pronounced that the child appeared in reasonable health. By then Cameron and Rachel had awoken and come to see what all the commotion was about.

Rachel said, 'I didn't know you were expecting Mum?'

Carol replied 'It's a long story we will explain later.' and looked up at me.

I decided there and then to take a day off work. 'It's an old story,' I said as I began to explain. 'It happened before I became involved with you.' By then the two kids were up and about and we decided to get them off to school before I would begin to tell the tale. That morning Bella had to make do with a quick trip around the garden. At half seven I went down to the front gate to await the Forestry Land Rover. When it pulled up I explained that we had trouble with one of the children and wouldn't be going with them that day. Later on Carol took the children to school in the Range Rover and I was left alone with the little one. Really I just didn't know what to do. Bella kept sniffing around us. I suddenly realised that we didn't have a cot or baby clothes and nappies.

Carol wasn't gone long and when she came back inside I began to reveal details about Mhairi. About her cave home in the mountains. About her strange isolated way of life. About our one night together and me discovering afterwards that she was pregnant. She listened intently without interrupting.

At the end of my explanation she said, 'Well you've certainly got yourself in a pickle now. What are you going to do about it?'

'At this moment I don't know,' I responded, embarrassed.

As usual women are more practical about these things. 'Well I think we ought to get her down to the Doctor, have her checked out. She may be ill or dying and that's why she was left here.'

We saw the district nurse first, the one who'd visited me and Carol before. After a thorough examination she declared that the baby appeared to be quite healthy. She was also able to provide us with some nappies and a baby's bib. Fortunately she didn't ask too many questions although we did tell her how we discovered her.

'I think she'd better see Doctor Masson,' she said, then went into his room when the previous patient had left. She was back out again in a few minutes. 'He'll see you now,' she said and ushered the three of us through into his surgery.

'Well you've got yourselves a problem I understand,' he began as he ushered us to seats.

I tried as briefly as I could to explain the situation.

'Oh her,' he replied shaking his head on my mention of Mhairi. 'We've all tried and given up with her.'

I went on to explain that our relationship was well over before I became involved with Carol and it was purely a silly one night fling.

'Do you know how old the child is?' he asked.

'She must be under a year,' I said.

'H'm. Sister tells me she is healthy but let me have a look.' Carol passed the baby over. He made various small tests and inspections. 'She seems all right to me. When did you last see Mhairi?'

'Over a year ago,' I replied. 'I could see then that she was pregnant.'

'Are you sure it's your child?' he asked.

'Pretty sure,' I said.

'The two of you have to decide pretty quickly what you are going to do with her. If the social people will let you, you can consider keeping her or if you're not she will almost immediately have to go into an infant's home. It's a tough decision for you to have to make.'

Carol and I looked at each other without making any comment.

Doctor Masson cut in. 'I'll telephone the social people now and I'll arrange for them to visit you this afternoon. Will you make sure you're in. I'll also get the nurse to see you all again at the end of the day.'

We agreed to that. On our way home we called in at the village store for Carol to purchase as many baby's clothes, nappies and requirements as she could put her hands on. In the afternoon a social worker rang to say she'd be over later to check over our situation and see if it was suitable for us to keep the child at home. By then we'd had a phone installed as Carol said she couldn't live without one. On arrival the lady wrote down details about us and inspected the baby. At the end she said, 'Well everything here seems fine as long as the dog accepts the child. If she doesn't, then one of them will have to go immediately. I am afraid you have a tough decision to make but you'll have to make it quickly because we can't let the uncertainty go on for more than a day or two.' With that she left.

Carol and I discussed the matter further. 'It's really down to you Carol,' I said eventually. 'I wouldn't be able to bring up a baby like this myself. I wouldn't have a clue what to do. And I have to go to work each day.'

She looked at me intently for a few moments but said nothing. Then she said 'I'll think about it. I'll let you know my decision by tomorrow.' We left it at that for the time being.

That day, as I was home, I went to the village to pick up the kids from school. By the time I got back the district nurse was in the bungalow with Carol inspecting the child further. 'She looks OK, but she needs to put on weight. She's too thin. She needs feeding up.'

'Her mother was like that. She never ate any solids.'

The nurse wrote down some additional food nourishments and supplements for us to buy for the baby and she had also found a carrycot for which we were grateful as Carol and I had already had an animated discussion on where we would have her to sleep.

That night Eilidh slept in the cot in our bedroom. I won't say it was the best nights sleep we had ever had. The baby gurgled on and off for most of the night. When she cried out Carol got up to deal with her and took her into the living room to attend to her.

In the morning we were all up early, I to take Bella out and deal with her and my breakfast before organising myself for work. Carol dealt with the baby and Bella sniffed around looking curiously on at this strange new being. 'If she becomes a problem you'd better put her in the outside shed,' I said referring to the dog.

'Do you mean the dog or the baby,' she responded instantly

'Have you had any thoughts on what we discussed about keeping her?'

'I have but I'll see how we get on today. The district nurse is coming this morning and I'll talk things over with her.'

And so I left for work with a lot on my mind.

*****

That afternoon when I got in from work I could hear the baby crying. I raced into the bedroom where they both were. Carol was dealing with the baby on the bed. It looked like she was changing her nappy. 'Is she all right?' I asked concernedly.

'Of course she's all right. Babies do cry you know,' Carol responded sarcastically.

I went into the bathroom, changed out of my forestry clothes and showered. When I came out the baby had stopped crying and was in Carol's arms.

'How did it go with the nurse?' I asked.

'Very good. We had a long discussion about Eilidh. She was very helpful.'

'And what do you think? Have you made any decision?'

'I think so. I am up for it if you are, but it's going to completely change our lives. Are you prepared for that. I always wanted a third child so I suppose this is the easiest way of having one as I haven't had to go through all the pregnancy bit.'

I laughed. 'At least this one will be my child. What about the other two kids? Do you think they'll accept her.'

'At the moment they are just fascinated by it all, but as you constantly say, kids will adapt to anything. I think Rachel loves her already, she wants to hold and cuddle her.'

'And Bella?'

'So far so good. She sniffs around a lot. The social worker is coming again tomorrow for our decision. I've told her to come about four o'clock so you can be here.'

'Ok,' I said and organised Bella for her afternoon walk. 'What do you think old girl?' I said to her as I fixed her lead over her head. She gave me a lick on my ear.

When I got home after work the next day, the social worker's car was in the drive and when I went inside she was already talking to Carol and taking notes. Eilidh was on Carol's knee. We exchanged greetings. I excused myself briefly, as I needed to use the toilet and wash my hands and face, then I sat at the dining room table still in my mud stained forestry clothes.

'I've been talking to Carol,' the social worker said. 'Now I want to hear your side of the story. Are you definitely sure you want to keep the child, because if you do you will be legally responsible for her. If you neglect her in any way you will be prosecuted. I will be coming over periodically for at least six months or so, to check on things.'

I hesitated for a moment before replying. 'Yes definitely,' I said eventually. 'I'm sure she is my flesh and blood so I am responsible for her. However Carol is the one who will have to do all the hard bits as I have to go to work every day. So if she is agreeable I certainly am.'

We both looked across at Carol who was bouncing the baby on her knee. 'I've told you I am,' she responded looking back at me.

'OK,' the social worker said. 'I'm afraid there are papers to complete.'

She bent down to her briefcase which was on the floor and pulled out a sheaf of papers. In all they took about an hour to complete. Carol and I had to sign some of them. As she left she said, 'I'll be back some time next week with your copies. Until then I wish you good luck with the little one.'

Carol and I were exhausted, but I took Bella out for her walk with a lot on my mind.

* * * * *

Looking back on it all with hindsight I can confirm that they were crazy chaotic days. Most times it was bedlam. Carol and I had to care for the baby, get the children off to school, get myself off to work and still do all the chores around the house and garden. Certainly my peaceful, isolated highland way of life was gone forever. In a way I think it was good for me as I don't think I was cut out to be a reclusive bachelor. Except for when she was out with me Bella tended to keep her head down and stayed in her bed most of the day. But she seemed to accept it all with good grace. There were no real problems with her and the children. One day the lady social worker came over from Fort William with the papers which declared that we were Eilidh's official parents and guardians.

On one Sunday morning I got up early at daybreak, about five thirty at that time of year, before anybody else was up. I made myself some toast and coffee and gave Bella her breakfast, then together we made for Sgurr Dhòmhnaill and the cave. Fortunately it was a dry morning and the forecast for the day was good.

It had been a long time since I'd been up there and Bella enjoyed the freedom. Thankfully, as there had been no rain recently the river was quite low so there was no problem in getting across it. However, it was still a tough climb.

From a distance I could see no activity around the cave and no fire smoke. I was puffing by the time I reached the overhang. I called out Mhairi's name but there was no response. Bella and I both scrambled up over the overhang to find the place deserted. No sign anywhere of Mhairi. Except for the remains of a previous fire and a few discarded items there was nothing. I checked down in the water cellar but apart from a few buckets the place was deserted. 'Well it looks like she's gone old girl,' I said to Bella. 'I wonder where.' I never found that out. Memories of her craziness came back to me as we both scrambled back down the mountain.

On the Monday, after work, I called in at Jack Banyard's police station and told him of the news. 'I'll put out a missing person's report,' he said, 'but I doubt if we will ever find her. She's probably at another hideout in the mountains somewhere. She's an odd one that one.' So I left it at that that, but I never heard another thing about her.

I am now resigned to being a family man and all that goes with it, but I still live in the glorious Western highlands and all it's splendour. When the domestic scene gets too much for me Bella and I head off for the mountains I love, but I will still never forget Anne, she is ingrained in the depths of my heart.

THE END

ABOUT RICHARD F JONES

Richard was born in North Wales. He has also lived in the highlands of Scotland, the Wye Valley, Spain and Majorca, places where his page turning novels are mostly set.

Milton Keynes UK
Ingram Content Group UK Ltd.
UKHW031905201124
451474UK00001B/118